The Right to be Forgotten

Kris Rogers

Cahill Davis
Publishing

Cahill Davis Publishing

The moral right of Kris Rogers to be identified as the Author of the Work has been asserted by her in accordance with the Copyright, Designs and Patents Act 1988.

First published in Great Britain in 2022 by Cahill Davis Publishing Limited.

First published in paperback in Great Britain in 2022 by Cahill Davis Publishing Limited.

ISBN 978-1-8381820-5-2 (eBook)

ISBN 978-1-8381820-4-5 (Paperback)

Cahill Davis Publishing Limited

www.cahilldavispublishing.co.uk

Prologue

The frozen countryside slides by the windows as the local bus makes its way cautiously up the hill. Her nose is resting against the window. Every time she breathes, a pattern forms on the freezing glass, leaving condensation trickling down the inside. If she cranes her head, she can see the entrance to her road as the bus heads out of Mary Tavy village, on the edge of Dartmoor. With only four buses a day, she has to time her journey to and from Tavistock carefully.

She makes her way unsteadily to the front of the bus, holding on to the tops of the seats to stop herself from falling as the bus lurches up the hill trying to keep a grip on the icy road. The driver barely acknowledges her as he stops the bus to let her off, and before she's fully clear, the bus moves off.

"Thanks for nothing," she mumbles to herself, regaining her balance as she prepares to walk across Dartmoor to the cottage she now calls home. She is breathing heavily through her mouth as she attempts to negotiate the frozen ground back to the cottage, pulling her bobble hat lower to protect her ears from the bitter air that is stinging the back of her throat. From the main road where the bus dropped her off, a narrow, tarmacked road crosses Dartmoor, connecting Mary Tavy to Brentor. During the winter, it is often impassable to normal road traffic. The cottage is at the end of a lane just off this road, about halfway between Mary Tavy and Brentor village. Waddling like a penguin, feet wide apart to stop herself from slipping, she sets off on the thirty-minute walk back to the cottage.

When she chose this place, Phil was amazed at her choice, but its very remoteness had attracted her. Phil, her old friend from university, had found three suitable properties that were available to rent immediately, but only this one had felt safe to her.

Once she reaches the front door, she rummages through her bag to find her keys. Her fingers, warm from the thermal gloves, pull back momentarily from the icy feel of the old metal touching her skin. She puts her key in the lock and pushes hard against the door with her shoulder, the wood swollen with the damp and cold. A wall of heat engulfs her from the wood burning stove as she closes the heavy wooden door on the frozen countryside. Letting out a sigh, she rests her back against the door, relieved that she's managed to negotiate another day without him finding her.

The cottage, a farm workers' cottage at one time, belongs to Jenny's parents, who own a farm nearby. Now, it's used as a holiday cottage during the summer, attracting a constant stream of visitors who enjoy walking the Dartmoor countryside. Phil introduced her to Jenny and her family as his cousin, Anna Brown, which meant he could rent the cottage for her without any questions. He's owned the café in which Jenny works in Tavistock for ten years. It converts into a bar come brasserie in the evenings. She felt a moment of disquiet on first meeting Jenny—the ease with which Jenny and Phil work together and their camaraderie initially suggested something more than an employer/employee relationship to her. Later, she was to learn that Jenny was his first and longest-serving employee.

Gradually, he had been introduced to her family, sometimes hosting family celebrations at the café or attending them by himself at Jenny's home. It was only later that Phil mentioned Jenny's partner Jez, who works for Jenny's parents on the farm.

Putting her bag down on the old pine table in the kitchen, she lets her gaze travel once again over her surroundings. The kitchen is basic but cosy with a wooden floor that has seen better days and functional cupboards in need of re-staining. The Belfast sink with its brass taps gives the kitchen a shabby chic feel rather than just shabby. The kitchen is the hub from which the other rooms in the cottage sprout like the branches of a tree. The front door opens into the kitchen with the stairs directly in front and the kitchen table snuggled under them towards the back of the room. An outside door on the far wall of the kitchen leads into a small courtyard where a brick-built outhouse covers the oil fuel tank. Next door to it is another old building which houses the washing machine and a tumble dryer. To the left as you enter the kitchen is a pine door that leads into the sitting room—a perfectly square room with the same wooden flooring as the kitchen. The room is sparsely furnished with not much more than a sofa and a bookcase. All the furniture, including the small TV and the short wooden stand it sits on, looks as though it's been well used but carefully looked after. It makes her think of the junk shops she used to visit on weekends when she was trying to furnish her first flat. Nothing matches but that somehow doesn't seem to matter. Instead, it gives the cottage a warm, comfortable ambiance that's often lacking in holiday accommodation.

Upstairs, the main bedroom is large and airy and the walls are painted white, the floorboards left bare, giving it a homely yet functional feel. The black wrought iron Victorian fireplace on the back wall of the room looks like an original, and an old wooden blanket box rests in the corner, perfectly positioned to allow the occupant a seat to admire the view from the front of the house following the road across Dartmoor. Next door is a smaller bedroom painted in sky blue, with bunk beds and a small chest of drawers. This window overlooks the outbuildings to the side of the cottage.

She stands at the window in the main bedroom for a moment, absorbing the view across Dartmoor; the Brentor road leading up a hill and then meandering out of view. She can see the farm in the distance which belongs to Jenny's parents. Sheep are scattered across the landscape, and although she can't see them from here, she knows that a breed of highland cattle also live here thanks to the one she encountered on the road to the cottage a few days ago. She'd been for a walk to explore her surroundings and on the way back there it was just standing in the road, blocking her way. It looked ferocious with its big shaggy head and horns, but as she carefully circumnavigated it, it moved away without giving her so much as a backward glance.

As she's gazing out the window, large, heavy flakes of snow begin to drift down, increasing in speed, giving the illusion of a veil descending from the shadowy sky. A car drives slowly along the road towards Brentor village, its headlights glowing through the gloomy, snowy countryside. She follows its progress for a minute before turning away from the window and making her way back to the kitchen.

Switching the radio on in the kitchen brings a sense of outside life into the silence of the cottage: she can no longer hear her own breathing or the old Napoleon clock she wound when she first arrived ticking in the sitting room. A distant memory of her grandparents' house and a similar clock come flooding back as a familiar chime extols the hour. It's comforting to hear it during the night when she can't sleep, the reassuring sound of it gently ticking away in the background like a human heart. It makes her feel less alone somehow, as if someone else is living in the cottage with her.

The next day, she wakes to an eerie opal light illuminating the bedroom. Although it is scarcely dawn, it's so bright that there's no need to click the bedside light on to see what time it is. She swings her feet out of bed, grateful for the large wool rug she purchased from the pannier market in Tavistock, and pads over to the window. Pushing back the thin cotton curtains, a thick blanket of fresh snow covering the white winter landscape is revealed. She opens the window and leans out so that the bitterly cold air winds its way around her painfully thin body, into the room. It's completely silent—no birds, no sheep, no highland cattle. No car tracks or footprints in the snow. She's the only living thing as far as the eye can see. Even the farm buildings have blended into the landscape, camouflaged by the snow, beautiful and lonely. Closing the window, she pulls her dressing gown off the hook on the back of the door, feeling the soft, fluffy material as she wraps it around herself, reminding her of when she used to bury her face into the soft fur of her old cat. A fresh wave of grief assails her as she leans against the wall halfway down the stairs, trying to block out the last image of Fifi, her beloved companion. Wrapped in a blanket at the vets after being run over, her wide eyes slowly beginning to cloud as the vet administers the drug to put her to sleep. Holding her tightly as she slips away, willing Fifi to feel all the love she holds inside for her. Wiping her wet cheeks with the back of her hand, she pulls the dressing gown tighter around her before heading into the kitchen to turn the heating up and make her first coffee of the day.

Later, as the sun tries to make an appearance in the white-grey sky, she shovels snow away from her front door where it's formed a snowdrift. Luckily, the back door is sheltered and she was able to make her way to the outhouse to get a spade. The idea that she only has one exit route from the house if she needs it makes her feel uneasy, as it would be impossible for her to climb the wall at the back in her current condition. With some effort, using her shoulder, she manages to shove the front door open wide enough to squeeze through the gap.

Fifteen minutes later, sweating inside her thermal jacket, she stops shovelling the snow to give her aching back a rest. She has cleared an area in front of the door, but the snow is so thick it's like shovelling wet sand, and her jeans are soaked to her knees. Stretching her back, she freezes at the sound of an engine in the distance. She peers in the direction of the noise, eyebrow raised, trying to work out how even something the size of a 4x4 could drive through this snow. She chuckles softly to herself as a shape appears in the distance, coming down the hill. Of course. A tractor. As it gets closer, she can see that there are two people in the cab: Jenny's father and brother. She assumes they're probably out checking on their livestock.

Jumping down from the cab, Tim, Jenny's brother, wades slowly through the snow to greet her. "Are you coping ok? Is the electricity still on?" he asks as he reaches her side.

"Everything's fine here. Just trying to clear the snow away from the front so I'm not trapped if it starts snowing again."

A smile trembles on Tim's lips as he attempts to hide his amusement at her paltry efforts. "I wouldn't worry about that. We'll come and dig you out if needs be, but it will probably be gone in a few days anyway. Mum wants to know if you want to come back and stay in the main house until it starts to thaw."

"I'm fine, honestly; the solitude suits me."

"Well, give us a ring if you change your mind," he says, climbing back into the cab and waving as the tractor moves off in what she assumes to be their continued search for stray livestock.

Deep down, she wanted to accept the offer but knows she isn't ready for the probing questions that would have been thrown her way. Questions about why she's here and maybe even prying into her past. No, she needs to sort her story out first. Phil cobbled together a brief summary to cover her presence at the cottage but it won't bare scrutiny if someone starts probing too deeply. Standing there in the freezing snow in the middle of nowhere, she begins to realise the enormity of what she did.

She struggles to breathe in the dark tunnel that transforms into her coffin as she fights through the dense layers of darkness to consciousness, unable to use her arms, which are tied behind her back. Thick, black tape covers her mouth from ear to ear, and her feet are tied at the ankles with plastic tags that bite into her skin every time she tries to move. She's wedged tightly into the dark, narrow space. A foul smell penetrates her nostrils as she tries to regulate her panicked breathing. A clear plastic bag suddenly floats into view, slowly hovering over her face before falling, settling over her nose and taped mouth, clinging to her skin like a mask. The cold, hard stone penetrates the thin material of her clothes. An image of her mummified body moulded into the stone floor emerges out of the gloom below her. NO. The floor comes into focus, level again with her limited vision, digging into the bones of her hips as a heavy weight presses into her chest. Her brain screams for help to her body as it starts to lose track of thoughts and jumble what could only be memories. Inside her head, a small, yellow light appears in the distance, growing larger and brighter as it moves steadily towards her until it's suspended above her. The light falters, glowing intermittently, a lighthouse in the fog. A long strip of dark material slowly starts to wrap itself around the light, creating a whipping sound inside her brain, cutting like a blade through her faltering senses. She scrunches her eyes and tries to move her hands to cover her ears as if that will somehow protect her against the internal noise. But her hands are still tied and her wrists sting against the movements. The wrapping motion is getting faster and faster now, whipping around the light until it is completely extinguished, leaving her in complete silence and darkness. She knows that she is in a bad place, hovering between life and death. A thin, piercing scream cuts through the silence…

Her own scream. Her eyes shoot open, heart feeling like it's trying to hammer its way out of her chest. She's bathed in sweat, hair clinging to her face, pyjamas damp against her body. Throwing the duvet back, she struggles to sit up and breathe. She looks around the room to reassure herself that she's awake, she's ok, she's free and she's definitely in the bedroom of the cottage on Dartmoor. She can feel her heartbeat start to slow now.

A cold shiver takes hold of her body as she stumbles out of bed, wrapping her dressing gown tightly around her thin frame with its slightly swelling stomach. There are no lights on Dartmoor and it's still dark but the blanket of snow illuminates the landscape. There has been a fresh fall overnight, so the tractor's tyre tracks are barely visible under the new layer. She's ok. She's safe here. No one can reach her tonight.

Chapter One

Milly: Before

" It's your turn to switch the alarm off."

"Mmm... you do it." Keeping my eyes tightly closed, I snuggle further under the duvet.

A sigh, then Dan gets out of bed to kill the alarm clock. We keep it on the windowsill, ensuring one of us has to get up to turn it off. And whoever that someone is also has to make the morning coffee. I still haven't opened my eyes as he pads downstairs. Smiling to myself, I hear the noise of the kettle being filled.

I must have dozed off again, as a few minutes later, the smell of coffee is prickling my nostrils, a hand gently squeezing my shoulder.

"Wake up, lazy bones."

It takes a while to prise my eyes open, but when I do, Dan isn't in the room anymore.

I'm still in bed, drinking my coffee when he emerges naked from the shower, wet, blonde hair sticking up at all angles. I follow the movement of the muscles in his back and shoulders as he blow-dries his hair. He watches me in the mirror, a smile playing on his lips. He hasn't yet lost the gym-honed body he gained in the army despite working as an IT specialist for a security firm for the last year. I pull a face as he rolls his eyes at the sight of me still in bed.

"Are you going to grace work today with your presence?"

"Do you fancy going to the pub for something to eat tonight?" I ask hopefully, ignoring his question and his sarcasm.

"Yeah, I should be home by seven." His reply is automatic, distracted, as he runs his hands through his fine, blonde hair, giving it the appearance of a style that doesn't try too hard, his mind already on the day ahead.

I untangle myself from the quilt to start getting ready for work.

"Well, that's just great," I mumble to myself as half my Hobnob biscuit breaks off and falls into my coffee. Colin pauses, momentarily losing his trail of thought as he runs through the schedule for the afternoon.

Colin and I first crossed paths just over six years ago when I was fresh out of university with a vague idea that I wanted to work for a charity but with no idea what that entailed. I applied for an administration job with a charity where Colin was the head of fundraising. I got the job, and two years later, Colin was appointed as the CEO of a small local charity. He asked me to go with him, and I jumped at the offer.

The first four months I worked with Colin, I had a massive crush on him, spending more time than I'll ever admit fantasising about him. Knowing him so well now, I realise how amused he must have been by my behaviour. I feel my cheeks redden as I think back to how obvious it was that I had a thing for him. He handled it sensitively, letting me know he had a boyfriend and cracking a joke that if he swung my way, I might have been in with a chance. I was invited to his house for a meal one night to meet his partner, Ben. I have no clue why I actually went, considering he must have warned Ben about my... abundance of affection for him. But I'm glad I did. Despite my disappointment, I couldn't help but like Ben immensely, so much so that when I was looking for somewhere to live, he suggested I rent their basement flat. I lived there until I met Dan and moved in with him.

Colin is notoriously untidy and his desk reflects this. It's covered in files, bits of paper, dust and other unsavoury debris.

I perch my coffee and another Hobnob on the edge of his desk. Colin likes to do a quick briefing before any outside event. As I'm the only one attending today's event, this chat will be very quick.

"So," he says, breaking off half my Hobnob, "are you ok with Sidney's costume in this heat?"

I think about the costume: Sidney the Snail, our charity mascot. Unfortunately, a full-length costume. But after the children of this primary school nominated our charity to receive a donation, I can't let them down at their own school fete.

I sigh. "I'll be fine as long as I don't have to wear it for more than an hour. Maybe he can just make a special guest appearance before departing. Then, I can reappear as myself for the rest of the afternoon. What do you think?"

"That should be ok," he says, smiling, no doubt secretly relieved he won't have to be the one wearing the costume.

The T-shirt I'm wearing under the costume is soaked with sweat, clinging to my back and chest, sweat also trickling down my forehead and the sides of my nose. I'm glad I sprayed myself with perfume before putting the costume on; at least there's a nice smell inside the musty head. I glance towards the church clock just visible down the lane. Five more minutes until Sidney is due to depart.

I feel a tug on the back of Sidney's shell and groan. It's surprisingly difficult to manoeuvre in this costume. I almost overbalance as the persistent tugging pulls me backwards. Steadying myself, I carefully turn, checking to see what I've managed to hook the back of the costume on.

"Can I have a selfie?" a little girl with a cheeky grin asks, holding her phone out to me. I pose beside the girl, holding the phone at arm's length.

"Do snails have arms?" she asks suspiciously, trying to catch me out.

"Not normally," I say in Sidney's best gruff voice, "but I'm a magical snail."

She seems to accept this before running back to her group of friends.

Three minutes to go.

I release a long breath and take a moment to close my eyes once I finish peeling off my T-shirt in the gym changing room. I quickly pack Sidney's costume into its bag and get changed into a loose-fitting cotton dress. Another spray of perfume to freshen up, although the sharp hint of sweat still clings to me. I run my fingers through my short, damp hair, unsticking it from my forehead before quickly towel-drying it and adding a few squirts of dry shampoo. I'll pass muster at the cheque presentation—just.

Sometimes, I feel as if I'm getting too old for this job, with thirty looming fast on the horizon. I should be looking for another career. A career that pays better. I've been hoping for a promotion but, realistically, there are no promotion prospects. And I don't know how much longer I can keep feeling ashamed for having to rely on Dan to cover the majority of the household bills. To his credit, he never mentions it. Maybe he doesn't want to add to the shame I already feel by bringing it up. Or maybe he knows that my job provides me happiness and that matters more to him than what I could gain elsewhere financially. Either way, for myself, I know I need to stop coasting.

Deep breath, mindfulness, here I am, concentrate. I push the door to the gym open. The sultry midday sun makes the air feel like a sauna as I walk towards the crowd to mingle at the fete.

After enduring what felt like forever but was realistically an hour in that damn costume, I'm relieved to be on my way home. I didn't stay at the fete for long after my mascot appearance, desperate to reach my shower as quickly as possible. I wind my window down and let the breeze run through my hair as I drive.

The lights change to red as I approach the roundabout. Slowing, I move into the left-hand lane and stop behind an old Vauxhall Astra. My neck is aching from the surprisingly heavy weight of Sidney's head, so I lean back on the headrest to ease the tension and close my eyes for a minute. A red haze penetrates my closed eyelids as the sun beats down on the windscreen.

The traffic lights are still on red when I open my eyes. I ease my foot off the brake, ready to move. A car pulls up sharply beside me, and I can hear a police siren somewhere in the distance. Shaken out of my own little world, I glance to my right, to the passenger side of a dark blue car, directly into the eyeliner-smudged, tear-stained eyes of a woman. She holds my gaze with a pleading look as she slowly mouths: *please help me*. Her coral-painted lips exaggerate each word, the last one barely seen as the lights change and the car quickly pulls away, a flash of her blonde hair the last thing I see of her.

My mouth has dropped, my hands shaking on the steering wheel. What's happening to her? Has she been kidnapped? The car behind me beeps its horn, jolting me from my thoughts. I press down on the accelerator and enter the roundabout. A little voice in my head tells me to follow. No, I should go home. I will go home. I heard sirens— maybe that's the police searching for her. Get home, ring them, tell them what you saw. They'll deal with it.

I don't even realise I've changed lanes until I pass my exit to follow the other car. The misery in her blue eyes has burned itself into my brain, compelling me to follow her like a magnetic force. *It's not too late to turn around*, I tell myself. And yet I still don't. I can't call the police or anyone. I should have listened to Dan about getting handsfree.

There are two cars between me and the blue car which I now recognise as a Golf. With my heart hammering so hard in my chest that I can hear the blood pulsating in my ears, I still have no idea what I intend to do other than keep the car in sight. If I follow it to its destination, then what? What if the destination is hundreds of miles away? Will I still follow?

The traffic slows, and I realise the Golf is turning off to the right. I put my right indicator on. As it roars off down the straight road, I take my chance with the traffic, cutting across an oncoming car as I turn to follow. The sound of a car horn follows me as I push harder on the accelerator, trying to keep the Golf in view. I'm fairly knowledgeable when it comes to cars due to Dan being a bit of a petrolhead. Although my car is an old model, I probably have a similar size engine, so it's not too hard to keep it in sight.

The car slows, approaching a junction, allowing me to catch up. I can read the number plate clearly now. I repeat it over and over, trying to imprint it into my brain until I can write it down, mentally mapping the route at the same time. My right hand's tightly gripping the steering wheel as I accelerate through the gears to catch up. *Not too close*, I tell myself. We appear to be heading for the M1. Should I pull over to call the police or should I keep following? I'm still kicking myself for not having handsfree.

As we approach the M1, the rush hour traffic is already building, slowing the traffic until it comes to a halt. I'm right behind the car now and can see the back of the girl's head. She turns her head to the left, maybe looking in the wing mirror. I hope she knows I'm here.

Rummaging in the passenger footwell for my bag while keeping one eye on the road, my hand finds my mobile. I text the registration number to Dan. He won't know what it means, but he's not due home from work until late, so he won't be wondering where I am or what's going on yet.

Dropping my phone on the floor as the lights change, I accelerate down the slip road and onto the motorway. The Golf is moving fast but has to slow to join the carriageway as I move in quickly behind it. The girl's head is facing forward again. The Golf overtakes the car in front, and I follow into the middle lane and then again into the fast lane as we accelerate up to eighty miles per hour. The traffic ebbs and flows. I manage to keep the Golf in view as we approach a junction, speeding past it, my heart hammering above the noise of the engine. As we approach another junction, the Golf begins to slow and move over to the inside lane, indicating to come off. I start to slow and move over too. Where is the driver going?

We join the A45. Two lanes now. I'm still on the inside, but the Golf is pulling away in the outside lane. I wait for an opportunity to pull out and follow. I can still see the Golf three cars in front of me as we head past Northampton and out towards Wellingborough. I'm so stressed I can hardly breathe. Taking a few deep breaths, I wipe each of my sweaty hands in turn on the skirt of my dress while keeping a hand on the steering wheel.

We come off at Wellingborough and follow the route around the town, heading out towards Kettering and eventually the A14 to Corby where we merge onto the A43. I nearly lose the Golf a few times in the rush hour traffic.

Starting to shake with the stress of it all, my right leg cramps. Stifling a cry, I try to flex my leg without taking my foot off the accelerator, but the muscle seems to be tightening rather than relaxing. I'm not sure I can manage this for much longer. The Golf suddenly pulls onto an estate road without indicating and accelerates out of sight. With part of my focus now on my cramping leg, I nearly miss the exit. I find myself on a large housing estate with many side roads leading off to similar looking roads. I bite my lip. *Where did you go?*

After a fruitless five minutes of driving around the estate, I catch sight of the blue car parked down a side road. Quickly checking my rear-view mirror, I swing my car in an arc, accelerating back to the turning. I slow as I see a man emerging from the car. Baseball cap. Grey tracksuit. I'm looking for a space to park further down the street, all the while watching the car in my rear-view mirror. I reverse into a space at the side of the road.

I can see the girl in my wing mirror, walking up the drive, ahead of the man, to a terraced house. She stumbles as the man puts his arm around her waist and then they are inside the house and gone from view. I reach for my phone, which has slid under the seat, patting the floor until I feel the plastic display, cool on my fingertips. With shaking hands, I manage to tap nine-nine-nine.

"Please hurry, I think something awful is about to happen."

The operator takes what feels like an age to establish the facts after I've gabbled out my story. Ten minutes later, I'm still waiting for the police to arrive even though she assured me someone was on the way. I phone again and go through the same painful process. She again assures me that a patrol car is nearly with me.

As I end the call, I notice a text from Dan: **What?**

I haven't got time to explain now.

My hands clasp the steering wheel, eyes glued to the rear-view mirror framing the house. The front door stays shut, and the windows glint at me with the remains of the warm September afternoon sun. I know that I have to do something.

Click. The driver's door opens, and although I'm the one who's opened it, it still makes me jump a little. Shaking with nerves, my legs feel unsteady beneath me as I get out of my car to approach the front door. Arms wrapped tightly around my chest, fingers clinging to the cotton of my dress, I force my legs to walk up the drive. One wobbly step after another. Before I can think it through, I'm knocking on the front door which hardly looks white anymore under all the dirt. I look around frantically for a doorbell, but there isn't one. The house remains silent, the door remains closed. The grainy net curtains at the downstairs window look as if they could do with a wash. I knock harder in case my first knock was too timid, and I swallow hard, realising I have no idea what I'm going to say if anyone actually answers.

The sound of an engine approaching distracts me, and I turn to see who it is as a police car pulls up at the kerb. Oh, the relief as I find myself running down the path towards it.

"I can't get a reply," I cry as I reach the two police officers getting out of the car. My voice sounds alien to me: high-pitched, way beyond the verge of panic.

The younger policeman approaches the front door as the more fatherly looking one places a hand on either side of my shoulders.

"Calm down and tell me what happened."

I realise I'm hurling information at him at a hundred miles an hour, my words all jumbled into one long incoherent sentence. From the corner of my eye, I can see the other policeman looking through the front window as I try to concentrate on the kind face of the man in front of me. His voice seems to be coming from far away.

The younger policeman looks towards us, shaking his head. "There's no reply. Are you sure they're still in there?"

"No one's come out," I croak, my lips sticking to my teeth from lack of saliva.

The younger policeman bangs on the door again. "Open up, this is the police."

Still nothing.

"Ok, let's see if we can break in."

A neighbour appears from the house opposite. She looks dressed for work in a smart skirt and waistcoat. Her long, dark hair is tied back in a chignon, her makeup perfect. "No one lives there," she shouts from across the road, one hand on her car door, ready to get in.

The fatherly policeman goes over to talk to her. I nibble on my nails as I wait for them to finish their hushed conversation.

Leading her back across the road with him, she catches my eye as he tells me, "This lady says it's a rented house. It's not occupied at the moment."

His colleague is heading to the car. "Let the station know we are going to force entry." He gets a battering ram out of the boot.

The neighbour and I stand and stare. I'm shaking uncontrollably now, my teeth chattering with tension and nerves. There's a sick feeling deep in my stomach. Internally, I realise that I'm preparing for the worst. The driver hiding in the house, hunted down, shouting, fighting as he resists arrest. The dead or dying body of the girl.

The door springs open with a loud crack as it hits the wall inside.

They enter, calling, "Police! Is anyone here?" Then, the sounds of heavy footfall and doors opening as they make their way through the house, checking each room.

Minutes later, they re-emerge through the damaged front door.

The house appears to be empty.

Chapter Two

Hope: Before

As I approach the end of our road, I can see that my husband's car is not on the drive. I let out a slow breath, the tension draining out of me. The sad thing is, I didn't realise how anxious I was until that moment of relief. I'm becoming conditioned to living like this: tense, watchful, careful how I choose my words, self-editing my conversations when I'm around him. The only time I can relax at home is when he is not there.

I carefully park my car on our drive, making sure I'm exactly aligned with the left panel of the garage door so he doesn't have a chance to start complaining that I haven't left him enough room on his side of the drive. Cutting the engine, I sit motionless in the car for a few minutes, enjoying the solitude. The metallic noise of the magnet in the cat flap brings me out of my reverie. A little tabby head appears through the flap and meows in my direction.

Taking a deep breath, I get out of the car and let myself into the house. It shouldn't be like this. Why should I be nervous entering my own home? There was a time when I loved coming back to my cosy nest, but that was a different house and another life.

Last night was particularly bad. I arrived home late from work to be greeted with a surly face. Guy immediately demanded to know where I had been and why I hadn't phoned despite the fact it was only 6:30 p.m. I'd been stuck doing paperwork at the lettings agency I work at. I felt the tension building inside me as he refused to accept that I couldn't have arrived home earlier. Didn't I realise it was our wedding anniversary and he was going to cook me a meal? My suggestion of going out only made things worse, him calling me ungrateful, spoilt and a spend thrift.

"Easy come, easy go, that's you," he snarled, pointing to a saucer on the kitchen windowsill that I'd used to support a potted plant, insinuating that I didn't respect his property. An argument we'd had many times. I'd slipped up. When we first married, I assumed we would share household items we'd accumulated before we got together. Little did I realise he expected me to ask permission to borrow or use anything he considered to be his. I'd stupidly accommodated that quirk. My mistake was that I'd thought this was a saucer we'd bought after we had married. Apparently, I was wrong. The constant walking on eggshells that constituted my side of the relationship was making me ill. I listened quietly as he droned on. Part of me wanted to slap him and tell him to grow up but I knew that would escalate things to another level of abusiveness.

"Didn't you realise it was one of mine?" he demanded to know despite the fact we have more saucers between us than we know what to do with.

"I'm so sorry, Guy. I'll buy you another," I said, wearily. We've had so many rows like this, I've given up the futile task of trying to defend myself.

"You're just selfish and careless with my possessions." He followed me as I tried to leave the room. "Easy come, easy go, that's you," he shouted, picking the saucer up and smashing it on the kitchen floor—something he's done so many times that I no longer react to it. The cat ran upstairs. I quickly and silently followed her, leaving him standing there fuming. As I started to get changed out of my work clothes, I was acutely aware of the sound of him clearing away the broken saucer downstairs.

I locked myself in the bathroom and sat on the closed toilet seat, trying to compose myself. One deep breath, two deep breaths... My stomach clenched as his footsteps started up the stairs. I flushed the loo as camouflage before opening the door to face him. But he walked straight past, into our bedroom.

"Why can't you tidy up after yourself? Lazy cow leaving everything strewn across the bed," he shouted.

"I was just about to tidy up. I needed to go to the loo first." I deliberately kept all emotion out of my voice, not wanting to antagonise him further. It wasn't to be.

"You lazy, slovenly bitch," he spat, picking my work clothes off the bed and stomping downstairs with them in his arms. I heard the back door opening and the noise of the plastic dustbin lid slamming closed. Only my tights had escaped his wrath and lay forlornly in a heap near the top stair, looking how I felt: crumpled, despondent and unloved.

I didn't much feel like celebrating a wedding anniversary for a marriage I wished I'd never got into. I would get my clothes out of the bin later when he was calmer.

I realised I was trembling slightly even though I'd conditioned myself to not react to his outbursts. I felt like a robot, focused on controlling my own emotions in order to keep his as calm as possible.

Picking the cat up off the bed, I cuddled her, whispering soothing words, letting the feel of her little soft body in my arms calm me as I buried my face into her fur. After a few minutes, I went downstairs to face him. He seemed calmer, and I tried to relax a little. I started setting the dining room table, the familiar routine bringing a little normality to the tense atmosphere, but then he noticed we were out of the olive oil with garlic that he liked to cook with, and he turned to face me, eyes piercing straight through me.

"How can I be expected to cook if you don't keep the cupboards stocked?"

"I'll go out and buy more. It's ok. It's all good." I tried to diffuse the situation, unable to stomach the sound of his voice any longer.

I reached for my car keys. Just as my hand gripped the cold metal, he grabbed my arm roughly and started bundling me towards the front door.

With his temper in full flow, he shouted, "If you want to go, then get out, go on, get out."

"What are you doing? Let go," I cried out, trying to resist his hold. I winced as he strengthened his grip on my arm.

His fingers dug painfully into my shoulders as he opened the door and tried to push me out. I attempted to grasp hold of his shirt for some grip, but he grabbed my wrist, twisting it painfully, and used the full force of his body to shove me outside, slamming the door on me.

I silently stared at the closed front door, with my car keys in my hand. Shell-shocked, I remained stood there for a moment, half expecting him to open the door and apologise. I lifted my hand to knock gently, my heart beating into a panic.

But then a little voice inside spoke up, "This is your chance, go." I dropped my hand to my side.

Shaking badly, my wrist throbbing painfully, I could hardly operate the remote lock on the car. My wrist felt weak and uncoordinated. With trembling hands, I eventually managed to open the door.

Turning the engine on, I took a deep breath to control the shaking as I reversed out of the drive and made it to the road. Then, the front door opened. Guy came charging out and tried to open the passenger door, his big angry face filling the window... Until his big angry face became small and frightened. Then, he ran to the front of the car, hands on the bonnet, shouting, "Sorry. I'm sorry. I'm so, so, so sorry."

His temper always exploded and then subsided, leaving him full of remorse until the next time. For a split second, I considered running him over. Noticing our neighbour looking out the window and realising my cat was still inside, I obediently but reluctantly reparked the car on the drive.

Sick with tension, I climbed out of my car and entered the house. He started crying, apologising again.

"I will make it up to you with a lovely meal."

I sigh as I place my car keys on the table by the door. The trouble is, I've heard all this before, too many times now. I don't love him anymore. Deep down, I know that one slip on my part and I might end up dead one day. Somehow, I can't quite admit this out loud to myself yet.

I can't go on like this.

I feel so trapped.

Chapter Three

Kate: Before

"Wake up, Mummy." Little fingers prise open my eyes so that the light from the window seeps into my vision. Two big brown eyes stare at me, inches from my face.

"It's not time to get up yet, Chloe." I blink groggily at her.

Climbing on the bed, she sits on top of me, determined to stop me going back to sleep. "Timmy's been sick on my bed."

Timmy, our sixteen-year-old cat, used to sleep with Jamie and I but has recently taken to wandering around during the night.

I sigh and drag myself into an upright position. "Ok, ok, I'm awake. Now, are you going to get off me or what? I can't do much with you sat on me."

Chloe grins and slides off the bed, waiting impatiently at the doorway as I rub my eyes, yawn and depart from the cosiness. She pads along the corridor in front of me on her tubby five-year-old legs.

Jamie and I bought our three-bed Edwardian terrace house before we got married. What attracted me to it then— the original fireplaces, split-level bedroom layout and big old-fashioned bathroom—aren't very practical now we have two children.

Pushing open the door to Chloe's room, I can see the culprit snuggled at the bottom of her bed, his green eyes peering out of the once all black fur which now, in his old age, is speckled with faint traces of grey. He purrs softly in response to me stroking his head. Luckily, the sick is just a hairball and nothing major in size. As I lift Timmy up gently, he protests with a few small cries and a tiny swipe of his paw. I carry the warm, furry body to our room and carefully place him on the bed next to Jamie. I give him a little stroke, and he purrs softly in response as he goes back to sleep.

Having changed the duvet on Chloe's bed, she then decides she wants her breakfast, so at 6:15 a.m., here I am having my first coffee of the day while she eats her Rice Krispies, the washing machine rattling in the background with the offending duvet cover inside.

Thankfully, my three-year-old son Oliver is still asleep upstairs having not woken to me stripping the bed or the noise of the washing machine, and I know for a fact Jamie is also still asleep because he could sleep through an air raid if one were to happen.

I feel a touch of guilt at the thought of Jamie… or rather, my lack of thoughts about him recently. We kind of fell into a relationship I didn't see lasting with each other. There was no great bolt of lightning to say this was "the one". At least, not for me. It was more of a friendship with extras.

We drifted along for a few years until Jamie asked me if I thought we should buy a house together instead of renting. It seemed the sensible thing to do, and I guess I hoped it might fix things between us, make me feel more secure and settled, so I went along with it. The house hunting and setting up house together kept us busy for a while. I enjoyed playing house but it wasn't enough to fill the small empty space that had taken up residence inside me.

It wasn't too long after that that I actually decided I was going to leave him. We were going to a restaurant after work one night. For me, it was a parting date. A chance for a final memory. I'd already planned what I was going to say to him once we went home. We had reached the stage where we didn't have much to say to each other, and I was wishing I'd brought a book to read when Jamie blurted out, "Why don't we get married?" Unexpectedly, what was going through my brain wasn't what popped out of my mouth. Maybe he only asked as something to say to fill the silence. Maybe he was as surprised as I was that I said yes.

As the wedding approached, I kept meaning to have the conversation about splitting up, it just always seemed the wrong time. The wedding preparations kept us busy for another few months, and when the day arrived, I actually enjoyed it. We drifted on for another year, and just when I decided I couldn't carry on like that anymore, I got pregnant with Chloe. And then Oliver. And they became the centre of my life. There wasn't much room left for Jamie. He was just there, in the background somewhere, steady and supportive.

To distract myself from my own thoughts, I check my phone. Just a couple of emails advertising ebook deals and a text from Hope saying she needs to talk to me this morning and can I come into the office before my property viewing. I bite my lip, wondering whether this is a serious talk or just a catch-up, but I can't change my half nine appointment or risk being late. I've already had to cancel once before on this potential client, and he's not the sort of client you want to lose. Hope will understand. She'll have to. We've both worked so hard to build our lettings agency into a profitable business.

Even so, as I go through my morning routine, the text hovers at the back of my mind like a dark cloud. Why would she have text me that at 2:30 a.m.? I send her a text to say I'll ring later.

I drop Chloe off at school and walk back to my car, pull my phone out of my bag and call Hope's mobile. It rings out for a bit and then goes to voicemail. I wait for the beep.

"Hi, it's me. I got your message. I'm on my way to Worthington Gardens to meet Paul Dyer. I'll be there in about ten mins, so I'll phone again when I get there. Is everything ok?"

I try her again when I arrive at my appointment, but once again it goes to voicemail. A creeping sense of unease crawls through me. Something feels very wrong about Hope's unavailability.

Paul Dyer was great to work with, and after we viewed the house together, we agreed business terms so that we could act as agents for all three of his houses. He had bought two other similar properties in the same street and was renovating them before putting them on the market to rent.

As I arrive at the office, Hope is pulling into her parking space beside mine. Her little white Fiat 500 always looks spotless, but today it's covered in mud as if she's raced through a field. We both get out of our cars at the same time. Even underneath all the carefully applied makeup, I can see her eyes are red and puffy, but what really draws my attention is the bluish mark on her right cheek. Her mouth wobbles as she tries to speak, and she swallows hard to compose herself.

"What on earth happened?"

"Guy." Her eyes are filling with tears.

"What about him?"

She shakes her head, the tears spilling down her cheeks.

I say nothing, putting my arm around her shoulders, guiding her inside.

Kylie, our administrator, looks up from her desk as we enter the room. She seems slightly startled, her eyes darting from Hope to me, and then she springs into action as she takes in the situation.

"I'll make you both a coffee."

"That would be really good, Kylie," I reply as I shepherd Hope to our shared room at the back of the office, shutting the door behind us.

"What's going on?" I ask once we're alone. I stand at the table, looking down at Hope, who's slumped in her chair, a strong feeling of unease in my stomach.

"I can't go on like this, Kate." Hope starts to cry quietly again. I've never seen her so upset before. My mind is rapidly running through all the scenarios that could have made her so distraught, but deep down I know what, or rather who, caused this.

I pull my chair up next to hers and put my arms around her. "Guy did this?" I ask gently.

Hope nods, her lips trembling as she tries to suppress the tears.

I've never liked Guy who, in my opinion, is a good-looking, controlling bully. Within four months of Hope marrying him, I sensed she was unhappy. She always passed it off as things turned a bit flat after the wedding whenever I'd approach her about it. Seeing her sitting here now, I could kick myself for not trying harder to get to the truth. From someone in a stale relationship, I eventually ended up putting it down to her being in a similar situation. Stale but with a big lump of control.

"I'm so sorry. I didn't realise things were this bad," I whisper, clasping her hands in mine. "What can I do to help? Do you want to come and stay with me for a while?"

"I can't. It will only make things worse. I need to sort it out myself." She takes a deep breath, rummaging in her shoulder bag for a tissue. "I'm thinking about giving notice to the tenant in my old house so that I can move back there."

"Worse? The only way things can get worse than this is if…" I trail off, not wanting to think about it. "Oh, Hope, please come and stay with us. Jamie will understand, and the kids will love it."

"I can't put your family through the backlash that will happen." Hope swallows, trying to control her breathing through the tears.

"I have to plan everything carefully. He won't just let me go quietly no matter how bad things are between us. He won't make things easy for me," she finally manages to say.

"*If* there's backlash, we will get through it together." I pause. "Are you afraid of him?" I try to keep my voice calm and gentle.

"I'm afraid of his dreadful temper. I should never have married him. I haven't been happy for a long time, but I've just kept hoping things will get better and making excuses for his behaviour," she blubbers. "It's a control thing. He can't help himself."

"'He can't help himself' is no excuse, Hope. You know that."

Chapter Four

Hope: Before

J ust as I swing my bag off my shoulder, there's a knock at the door. I drop my bag on the floor and walk back down the hallway, trying to work out if I've invited someone over and can't remember or if I've ordered something online recently. My mind reaches a blank on both. I open the door to find Eileen, our elderly neighbour, on the doorstep. It's not unwelcome for her to come round but unusual nevertheless.

Eileen was already an established resident when we moved into our house just before we got married. We exchange pleasantries whenever we happen to pass each other by but we're not what I would call friends. A lover of cats, having had a few herself in the past, Fifi often retreats to Eileen's garden for cuddles when Guy and I are having one of our rows. I dread to think how much time she must be spending there of late.

And that's when it hits me. The row. We've had a lot but our last one... I brace myself for what she's about to say.

"Hello, Hope..." She clears her throat as her eyes fill with tears.

"What's happened? Come in," I say, opening the door wider and stepping aside. Various scenarios flash rapidly through my mind. None of them what she tells me next.

"No, I can't. It's Fifi…" Unable to speak, she points to her front garden then begins wringing her hands together. She takes a deep breath to steady herself. "I think she's been hit by a car."

I stand still, taking in what she just said. Then, it hits me like a blow to the stomach. I grip the door frame to stop myself collapsing. Fifi. My Fifi.

"Take me to her." I doubt she hears me, as I'm already out the door, running towards her garden. I stand in the middle of the garden, eyes searching for her. Turning on the spot as my eyes continue to dart from place to place. Breathing coming out in short, sharp bursts.

I catch sight of Fifi resting next to a small tree Eileen planted last year. I dart over and drop to my knees beside her.

"Oh God, Fifi. You're not dead. You can't be dead," I cry.

I stroke her head gently with the back of my hand—she's still warm. She opens her eyes slowly to look at me and emits a faint little cry, trying to tell me something.

"What is it, my darling?" I whisper close to her face. There's no blood that I can see, but she doesn't seem able to move.

"I'll get a blanket," Eileen says, running to her car. I gently run my fingers over Fifi's back, trying to feel for broken bones. The faint little cry comes again before her head weakly drops back down. I look around frantically to see Eileen returning with a tweed travelling rug.

Together, we carefully wrap Fifi in the blanket, only her little face showing. She doesn't struggle or make a noise. I know that I'm losing her. I'm just about holding it together as Eileen drives us to the vets. Holding Fifi in my arms like a newborn baby, feeling her warm body close to mine, I try not to scare her by howling with the grief that is bubbling up inside me.

"Please don't go Fifi, I love you so much," I whisper over and over to her, not caring what Eileen thinks. "What will I do without you?" Her eyes are already starting to glaze over, and she lets out a deep sigh.

By the time we reach the vets' and carry her over to the receptionist, her body is limp in my arms.

"My cat's dying," I manage to croak to the young girl sitting behind the desk, my tears falling onto Fifi's fur.

She peers over at Fifi and immediately drops her pen. "I'll get a vet," she says, rushing off.

The vet ushers us into the back of the surgery, where I lay Fifi down on the examining table. The blanket is wet through, and her eyes are clouding over. I can already see the lack of any positivity on the vet's face as she bites her lip, already knowing the inevitable has happened. I turn away and face the clock tick tick ticking on the wall, unable to accept the look. Because Fifi is strong, Fifi is brave and only this morning she was rubbing her forehead against mine and purring away. She places her stethoscope against Fifi's heart anyway. It's not long before she moves it away and shakes her head.

"I'm so sorry…" she says softly.

But then Fifi's ribcage rises gently, and I gasp, ready to scoop her in my arms and take her home. My fighter. My beautiful girl. I feel a hand on my arm and turn to the vet. She shakes her head.

"That's just her body settling."

Eileen takes me in her arms as I emit a howl of intense pain.

It's quiet in the kitchen as Eileen and I sit opposite each other, nursing a mug of coffee each. The quiet is more comforting than awkward, just a reminder of how much Fifi means… meant to us. We both jump a little as the front door slams shut.

"Hope, what have you done with my gym bag?" Guy calls out. He stops in the doorway of the kitchen and raises an eyebrow. "Oh, hello, Eileen."

I can tell just by the set of his mouth, tight rigid smile and clipped manner of speaking that he's not pleased Eileen is sitting here in his kitchen.

"I'll leave you to tell Guy. Take care of yourself, Hope. I'll let myself out." She puts her mug in the kitchen sink and shuffles past Guy carefully, making sure not to accidentally touch him. I know she's never felt comfortable around him from the way her greetings are more short when we bump into her together.

Once Eileen leaves, Guy takes her seat, and I tell him the news. His reaction to the news is perfunctory in a "well, she was getting on in years" sort of way. He obviously felt he had to say something supportive but with minimum effort. To Guy, Fifi was just another reason to berate me. In a strange way, he's always been jealous of her, Guy always having to be the centre of my attention.

Guy stands, leaving me miles away in my head, my thoughts filled with scenes from Fifi's life. I somehow feel numb and miserable at the same time.

My attention shifts as I slowly become aware of Guy dropping things into the kitchen bin. Focusing more closely on him, I see two boxes of cat food in his arms.

Pain stakes me in the heart, as if I'm losing Fifi all over again. "What are you doing?" The words come out like the crack of a whip as the boxes hit the bottom of the bin.

He looks startled for a moment before replying. "I'm just clearing her things away so you don't have to do it. I thought the constant reminders might upset you."

"Well, they don't; they're comforting. Just leave everything." I look into the bin and almost cry out seeing her half a sachet of wet food in the bin, the rest of it having been eaten at breakfast. "I'll clear them away when the time is right," I snap. I snatch her water bowl from his hands and clutch it to my chest.

"When 'the time is right'? Is the time really ever going to be right? So, you're just going to leave everything lying around the kitchen until you decide it's ok to remove them?" he asks incredulously.

"That's exactly what I mean. Do you have a problem with that?" I ask sharply. I'm on a roll now, fuming at his audacity.

"It just seems a strange thing to do."

"Well, it's not, and if you ever loved Fifi, you would feel the same." Tears threaten at the back of my eyes as my throat tightens. If it wasn't for the fact I've already cried what feels to be every tear inside me, I would have erupted long before now.

"She was just a cat, Hope. And anyway, it will be a relief to get rid of the cat hair from my clothes." He chuckles as he gets the pet hair remover from the cupboard.

A stony silence descends upon the room. And that's when I feel it. Feel that the time is finally right. And not for getting rid of the pet bowls and food. I'm going to leave him. I'm more ready than ever.

"I've just lost my cat who's been my beloved companion for eighteen years and all you can think about is the cat hair on your clothes. Is your world really so narrow and self-centred?" I scream.

"You can talk. You and your precious cat. What a cliché. If I hadn't come along, what would have become of you?"

"How dare you," I hiss, all thoughts of tears now forgotten. "How dare you speak to me like that. At this moment, I can't imagine what I ever saw in you, but understand this: I don't intend to carry on like this for much longer."

"What does that even mean?" he sneers.

I move closer to him, my face now mere inches from his. "I'm going to leave you, just like Erica did."

The slap was hard and unexpected, bringing tears of a different sort to my eyes.

"You'll never leave me. You haven't the guts to do it."

Chapter Five

Milly: After

A noise similar to a coffee percolator breaks through my unconscious, sleep-drenched brain. *Bloody Dan,* I think, *why can't he sleep on his side?* Putting my hands on his shoulder and arm, I try to roll him over, but he's a dead weight and won't budge. "Wake up," I say, giving him a shake.

He does a loud snort as his eyes snap open. "Wha-what's the matter?"

"You're snoring again, and it's keeping me awake."

"Sorry," he mutters, sleepily rolling over so that his back is to me. It's not his fault really, it's just that I'm having trouble sleeping, and when I do finally nod off, he wakes me up.

With a sigh, I check the alarm clock: 2:30 a.m. I start to do the breathing exercises I found on the internet that are supposed to help you get back to sleep by concentrating your mind on your breathing to clear anxiety and worries. A bit like a form of meditation, I guess.

"What are you doing?" Dan's voice drifts over from his side of the bed.

"I'm doing breathing exercises to help me sleep."

"Well, can you do them more quietly?"

"What a nerve; you're the one who woke me up."

"You're clearly worrying about something. What's on your mind?" He turns over to face me and wraps an arm around my waist.

"I can't get that woman out of my mind."

Light fills the room as he switches the bedside lamp on. "I'll make us a cup of tea," he says with a yawn.

Half an hour later, still in bed, we've drunk our tea and I've gone through the sequence of events again with Dan.

"So, you definitely saw them go into the house?"

"Yes."

"The police couldn't find any trace of anyone having lived there recently, and the house has been empty and on the rental market for two months?"

I nod.

"What about the car? Did they find out who it belongs to?"

"A rental car. It's being rented to a man who lives further down the street. He works nights, and he parked it there in the morning when he came home from work. He was in bed when the police called to see him, and his neighbour said she had seen him return and that he hadn't been out again all day."

"Mmm but she can't be watching him all day, can she?" Dan slipped a reassuring arm around me. "I don't think you imagined it."

"The police seemed satisfied with him. They said they were puzzled and would have to check CCTV cameras on the route from where I first saw her. I haven't heard anything since. Do you think I should contact them to find out what's happening?" I realise I'm standing with my arms wrapped tightly around me in a defensive way. I wish I hadn't taken that self- awareness course; I am forever checking myself for the body language I'm giving off.

Making a conscious effort to relax, I say, "I can't get her face out of my mind. What if something really horrible is happening to her right now and no one is looking for her?"

"You've done everything you can. I don't think the police will tell you anything more at this stage."

"But where did they go? No one came out the front door. The back door leads into the garden. Maybe there was a door in the fence? Do you think he could have hidden her in the loft?"

"The police will have searched the whole house. She won't be hidden. They must have got out the back way somehow. The car is a funny one as well. Are you sure it's the same car you followed?"

"Yes, I texted the registration number to you. Do you think we should go back and talk to the man who is renting the car?"

"No." Dan looks at me sternly.

"But he might know something. Could he have given his spare key to someone?"

"If it's a rental car, he won't have a spare key. There is nothing more you can do. Leave it to the police."

"Mmm," I reply. I can tell he isn't going to change his mind on this tonight. Better to let him sleep on it.

Dan is soon snoring as I begin my breathing technique again. Just as I'm dropping off to sleep, an uneasy thought floats into my brain: maybe I'm not being taken seriously by the police. Perhaps they think I'm some kind of fantasist. But I did see her going into that house. I didn't imagine it.

I must get some sleep. Breathe in, one, two, three, four, five; breathe out, one, two, three, four, five; breathe in, one, two, three...

Chapter Six

Guy: Before

What began as a cynical ploy to get a woman into bed has turned into something more complicated. Life in London has become a mess: a failed marriage to the sought after, highly regarded Erica, followed by a series of short-lived relationships all going nowhere and a job which has hit a brick wall. You could say that I'm having a mid-life crisis in my early thirties.

If anyone asks—and they rarely do after the first few months—I always tell them Erica and I drifted apart, the marriage broke down slowly, it was long over when we finally separated, the separation was in effect pain free. A lie. No separation is ever pain free. The truth is more brutal than that.

Arriving home from work one night, I stepped on her keys as I opened the front door. I remember feeling puzzled as I bent to pick them up. I wondered if she had dropped them by mistake as she'd left the house that morning. The thought also occurred to me that she was late home, so maybe hadn't been able to get back in the house and was looking for her keys.

I sent her a text: **Your keys are at home. Where are you?**

Pushing the kitchen door open with my shoulder, briefcase in one hand, keys and phone in the other, I saw the envelope on the kitchen table. People talk about their heart skipping a beat in times of crisis, but I could have sworn mine actually stopped as I stood rooted to the spot, looking at that plain white envelope, my name written on the front in Erica's neat, upright handwriting. When my heart started beating again, I dropped my briefcase to the floor and placed my phone and keys on the table. Then, slowly, with trembling fingers, I reached for the envelope. It smelt faintly of Erica's perfume. I ripped the envelope open and took a deep breath as I unfolded the paper inside. In my heart, I knew what it would say before I read it, and I knew why she had gone. I just never thought she would have the guts to do it. I had misjudged her, and she had outmaneuvered me. I wouldn't let it happen again.

In the weeks after she left, I swung from feeling sorry for myself to absolute rage against Erica at the way she had left me. I tried to phone her a few times, but she blocked my calls. Friends and colleagues were sympathetic to me; I made sure I portrayed myself as the injured party. After all, she had left me and she wasn't there to defend herself. I may have insinuated that she was a high-maintenance personality and that she was involved with someone else with more status than me. Sometimes, I hated her so much that I was ready to tarnish her memory with any mud I could throw at it. In the quieter moments, I remembered how much I had loved her when we'd first met. I thought Erica would be different from the others, that she would set me free from all those confused feelings and emotions I'd been living with since hitting puberty, but, in the end, she was just like all the others. I needed someone to put me first. I wasn't prepared to play second fiddle to someone else's career, friendships or family.

Wow, she's beautiful—that had been my first thought when I'd met her.

"Guy, can I introduce you to my trainee, Erica Bowles?" Freddie had looked over her shoulder and raised his eyebrows as this vision of loveliness offered me her cool hand and her cool stare from her clear blue eyes. She'd smoothed a strand of her long, golden hair behind her perfect diamond-studded ear. I'd been smitten from the moment I met her. She was a star pupil destined to change her career from solicitor to barrister. I was a hotshot solicitor with a huge ego, a handsome face and big dick. We'd been attracted to each other. It was like a magnetic force field. The perfect wedding, the beautiful house, the luxurious holidays to expensive, exotic destinations. We'd had it all. And then she left me.

Five months later, with the house about to be sold, I was browsing through the job websites to fill a lonely evening when I saw a vacancy with a good firm in the Midlands, in a town close to where I grew up. It seemed like fate had intervened to show me a way forward while I took time out to take stock of my life and the type of person I was turning into. I wasn't sure I liked myself very much anymore. I'd assumed a more hard-bitten, arrogant persona since I'd qualified. I felt I was being tested and needed to prove myself in some way. Maybe this would be a chance to start again in a place that I felt a measure of security. Maybe a chance to find that bit of myself I'd lost in the relentless quest to make a success of my life. I wanted to break the pattern of self-destruction that was already beginning to form. If only I had been honest with myself or at least more self-aware, I might have been able to avoid the tragedy that was about to unfold.

Chapter Seven

Kate: Before

"Hope wants us to meet her new boyfriend. I thought I would invite them here for a meal, or do you think it would be better to meet at a restaurant?" Jamie doesn't appear to be listening to me. "What do you think?" I'm trying to suppress the irritation in my voice. Keeping one eye on the cheese sauce I'm stirring for the pasta, I look at him sitting at the kitchen table with Ollie beside him in his highchair.

Jamie is spooning food into a reluctant Oliver's mouth and trying to catch the overspills with the bib around Ollie's neck. Our kitchen diner is large enough to host a six-seater dining table with chairs and still have enough room left for a children's play area, an old sofa and a TV for the children to watch while I'm preparing meals.

Chloe is lying on the sofa, watching *Dora the Explorer* on the TV. It's the only programme that keeps her quiet. Sucking her thumb, she's completely entranced, dreaming of a time she'll have those adventures herself. Her free hand is dangling over the side of the sofa, absentmindedly stroking Timmy's head, where he has strategically positioned himself. My little girl, how will I really feel when she departs for her first solo adventure?

The couple who owned the house before us knocked through the kitchen wall, into the dining room. They obviously had a liking for vibrant colours, giving the kitchen a Mediterranean feel but without the weather to go with it. We keep meaning to redecorate but haven't got around to it.

"It would probably be better if we go out but that depends on if we can get a babysitter. Maybe your mum could stay over if she's free?" Jamie's voice cuts through my musings, bringing me back to the here and now.

"I'll ask her," I say, continuing to stir the sauce.

"What's he like?"

"He's a solicitor; specialises in corporate work. I met him briefly when he came into the office to sign the paperwork on a property he's renting. Very good-looking."

"Is that how Hope met him?"

Turning the gas off under the pasta, I notice Ollie has just spat his dinner all over Jamie's shirt. I hold back a huff, knowing I'll have to get it washed and ironed for him, ready for work tomorrow. I pass him a towel.

"He's just moved to the area after changing jobs. He works for Ellisons now. They've apparently been dating for about two months. She seems really keen on him from what I can tell."

Receiving no reply, I look over and see he's lost interest and is as focused on *Dora* as Chloe is. I roll my eyes and start to plate up dinner.

Having failed to get a babysitter, we're sitting around our dining table, making polite conversation with Guy Chambers. I'm studying him as he talks to Jamie about the Formula One season. Very good-looking doesn't do him justice. His thick dark hair is cut short, otherwise I think it might be inclined to be wavy; there is a hint of a curl on his forehead where his fringe is starting to grow out. He has a strong jaw, with the shadow of a heavy beard. He probably has to shave twice a day normally, but he's told us he wants to grow a beard, and I can imagine it will suit him when it's fully grown. His deep-set brown eyes are unnerving when he looks at me, making my stomach flip. On the rare occasions I've noticed a good-looking man staring at me, I've usually enjoyed the feeling, so why does it make me feel uneasy now? I get the impression he is playing with me.

Hope told me he used to be a rugby player and still has the physique of one. I'm attracted to him at first glance, but the longer he sits at my dining table talking to my husband, the less I like him. I can appreciate his physical attractions but there is something in his manner that sets me on edge. It's his voice, or rather the way he uses it, that puts me off. He has a habit of correcting Hope when he thinks she's wrong. Undermining her. Just little things like the way she pronounces a word.

"The food is lovely." Hope smiles.

"You're hardly qualified to comment," Guy jumps in. "I take over the kitchen when we are together. Hope's idea of a meal is baked beans on toast." A seemingly harmless joke but it makes me feel uncomfortable.

I glance at Hope as she rolls her eyes. "I'm not that bad," she says.

Surely, it's too early in their relationship for him to behave in this way? Although Hope doesn't seem to mind. Clearing away the dishes, I make a mental note to ask Jamie what he thinks later when we're alone.

"Where did you work before, Guy?" Jamie is asking him when I arrive with dessert.

"I worked for Askew, Morris & Co," he replies, naming a well-known London firm of solicitors.

"Why on earth would you leave there to come work in Warwick?" I ask in a conversational way. A slight narrowing of his eyes as they bore into me tells me he didn't take it in that way, but when he replies, his tone is friendly.

"I had the chance of a partnership. I'd never have been offered that at Askews. I haven't got enough capital to put into a partnership in a big city firm." He gives a little shrug, but somehow, plausible as it is, it doesn't ring true to me.

I've made a summer pudding and a cheesecake for dessert. He chooses the summer pudding, and I watch him separate the fruit from the outer layers, nibbling at it as if it could poison him. Jamie catches my eye, and I look away quickly before Guy notices.

"Would you like to try the cheesecake, Guy?" I ask.

"I'm not really a pudding fan. To be honest, I don't think this is baked properly." He points to his summer pudding with his fork.

There's a silence around the table.

Hope glares at Guy, her mouth starting to open.

"No problem," I say quickly before Hope has a chance to scold him. "Would you prefer cheese and biscuits?"

"What kind of cheese have you got?"

"Stilton or Cheddar?"

"I'll pass," he replies without even looking at me. He pulls his phone from his trouser pocket, leans his elbow on the table and starts checking his messages.

Hope looks so stunned that she's temporarily unable to react, then she quickly recovers herself, trying to fill the uncomfortable silence with chatter about how much she's enjoying her pudding and that it tastes fine to her. She's careful not to catch my eye, although I'm staring at her in disbelief.

"You're a hopeless cook, Hope, how would you know?" he says with a little chuckle.

The strained atmosphere follows us into the lounge, where I serve hot drinks. Jamie moves the side lamp so that

Guy can use the small table for his coffee. While Hope chats to me about Chloe, Jamie tries to make conversation about cars with Guy—the only subject he seems interested in other than work.

"We're thinking of changing our car for an SUV. Are you pleased with yours?"

"To be honest, I'm not really interested in the family car market; my car is just a way to get from A to B comfortably. I prefer high-performance racetrack cars."

The conversation isn't exactly flowing between them; I can hear Jamie constantly reaching for new subjects and being met by Guy's incessant negativity. I try to ignore it, carrying on my conversation with Hope. Jamie will have to cope with Guy on his own for a while.

As if he senses my want to avoid talking to him, Guy butts into our conversation as Hope is midway through a sentence. "Hope, where did you put my car keys?"

"I haven't seen them. You must still have them."

"No, I distinctly remember giving them to you." His voice, though calm, has a distinct edge to it.

"I haven't got them, Guy. You didn't give them to me." I can hear Hope trying and failing to conceal her irritation.

"I think you'll find I did." The ice in his voice turns the room chilly.

Jamie and I exchange helpless looks, both of us trying desperately to think of something to say to defuse the situation.

"We had better make a move anyway, Guy." Hope's mouth is set as she rummages through her bag, looking for the keys. "And, as I've already told you, I clearly haven't got your keys," she says brusquely.

"They are in your coat pocket," Guy states, refusing to let this go.

"Well, you must have put them there because I certainly didn't." She's facing him now, almost squaring up to him as if she's ready to take him on.

"Maybe they've been dropped somewhere," Jamie says before Guy can respond to Hope's challenge. He looks under the chair where Guy is sitting and emerges with a piece of Chloe's kitchen set while I migrate into the hall and retrieve the keys from the hall table.

Guy huffs. "Hope's always losing things. It drives me mad."

We say our goodbyes and close the front door as their car disappears down the road.

Jamie looks at me and raises one eyebrow. "That was hard work."

"Can you believe how he carried on?" I ask, leaning on the door, glad for the meal to be over.

"I can't understand why Hope puts up with it."

"She was probably just being polite for our sake. I can imagine they are having a monumental row now on the way home."

"MUMMY," Chloe shouts. I look up and see her standing at the top of the stairs. "You woke me up."

"You go and see to her." Jamie motions towards Chloe with his head. "I'll stack the dishwasher."

I put my arms around Jamie's neck, kissing him. "I'm so glad I'm married to you."

Chapter Eight

Erica: Before

I like the view from my kitchen window. The river scene overlooked by the Malvern Hills was the main selling point for me when Darren and I were looking for a house following the sale of our modern apartment. My preference is for a Scandinavian inspired interior and most English houses don't accommodate that style of living. It was a surprise and a relief when we found this place.

Sitting at the kitchen table, waiting for Hope to arrive, I watch a small cruiser slowly making its way along the river, a lone man at the helm looking completely relaxed and at peace with the world. Maybe we should invest in a boat. I'll mention it to Darren when he gets home. My large wall clock, the one that resembles a station clock, clicks onto the hour. She should be arriving now. I wonder again why I agreed to meet her. What could she possibly want from me?

Maybe it was that first conversation I had with her friend Kate that swayed me. It had come unexpectedly at work. My secretary is usually like a Rottweiler when it comes to vetting my phone calls. That day, she knocked before entering my office but didn't wait for a reply, which was highly unusual.

Not looking up from the brief I was reading as the door opened, I asked, "What's up?"

She told me, "I've just had a strange phone call."

Something in her voice made me stop reading and look up. Pam is always so calm and so in control. A bit like me really, which is probably why I chose her from the four others who came for the interview. She has an air of quiet efficiency that appeals to me. Over the last two years, there have been many occasions where I've been grateful for the choice I made. We've formed a bond, a good working relationship. She always has my back. I like to think we are friends.

That day, I could see no smile on her kind, motherly face. That was greatly concerning to me, as she can usually deal with anything thrown at her at work; she has to read a lot of disturbing material working for me, and her warm, friendly manner always takes the edge off the depravity and cruelty we are usually surrounded by.

"A woman phoned—a Kate Parkinson. She says she's a friend of your ex-husband's new wife."

"What? How bizarre. Does she want me to represent her? I can't do that," I said, puzzled at how I could possibly help the friend of the wife of my ex.

"She said she just wants to talk to you, about Guy. She's concerned for her friend's welfare," Pam said, shrugging.

I was tempted to just say no and have that be the end of it, but something stopped me. I told myself I was intrigued, maybe curious about the woman Guy had married after me, but really, deep down, I was worried.

I leaned back in my chair. "Ok, is she still on the phone?"

"No, I've taken her mobile number for you. I didn't think you'd want to talk to her without prior notice?" Pam looked at me quizzically over the top of her new slimline reading glasses.

"Thanks, I'll contact her." A sigh escaped me. Did I really want to speak to her?

"Have I done the right thing?" Pam stepped further into the room, taking her glasses off and looking at me through worried eyes. "I can get rid of her if you want?"

"No, it's ok, I'll call her back and find out what she wants."

As I swivelled my chair around to face the window, I watched the Big Issue seller standing outside the independent café we all frequented at lunchtime, engaged in conversation with a passer-by. He always has a cheery word for everyone even though he's usually ignored and has no choice but to stand outside in all weathers. I often purchase a copy of the Big Issue from him. A few months ago, he was featured in an issue himself and we had a conversation about how he ended up living on the streets. Even after all he'd been through, he was still so different from Guy...

Guy... I really have no interest in re-visiting that part of my life. It was a *big* mistake. One I've only just forgiven myself for. How was I to know it would end like that? Everything had seemed so normal before I married him. Or had it? Did I just ignore it? Make excuses for him? Brush it aside and under the carpet? I should have left it as a brief, exciting fling. I was so much younger then. You live and learn and hopefully move on to something, or someone, better. For me, something useful developed out of that period of my life. I hope I'm now making a difference to the lives of those women I've championed in court. I hope I've helped them to get closure and move on.

The sound of the doorbell suddenly cuts through the silence of the house. Even after all this time, I still appreciate the peace; not feeling on edge every time I hear his key in the lock or worrying about what sort of mood he will be in tonight.

A small blonde woman in a mid-calf length blue wool coat jumps back slightly as I open the door. She doesn't say anything and seems to be struggling to make eye contact with me.

"Hello," I say.

"Hello, Erica. I'm Hope. Thank you for agreeing to see me."

Chapter Nine

Kate: After

With my elbows on the desk, I cradle my head as I stare at the laptop screen. I've had to phone Jamie to get him to pick up the children tonight and give them their tea. I've just got so much to do here on my own. The website list needs updating but I just can't concentrate on it. It's been three days since Hope disappeared. Guy assured me he had reported her missing to the police, but they hadn't contacted me as I was certain they would have. I was, am, Hope's best friend and business partner. Why would they not want to talk to me? I will have to contact them. I need to know what's going on. I've phoned Hope's work mobile and private mobile constantly since she disappeared, but both are switched off. It's so unlike her; she never switches her phone off and always gets back to me within thirty minutes at most if I call.

I also tried to phone Guy several times, but it kept going to voicemail. Eventually, after I left a particularly desperate message, he did phone me back. He inferred that he really doesn't have the time to talk to me, as he has a lot on his mind. He left a silence hanging in the air, hoping I would take the hint and go away. I didn't.

Jamie pointed out this morning that maybe I just don't like Guy and that's colouring my view of the situation.

According to Guy's rather brief version of events, she went off in her car to work that morning and he hasn't seen her since. He said she seemed fine when she left. He wasn't worried when she didn't come home, as she'd said she was meeting a friend after work for a meal. He hadn't registered who she was meeting and in fact wasn't even sure she had told him. When she didn't come home by 10 p.m., he went to bed, as he had a breakfast meeting the next day and had to be up early. He must have fallen asleep, as the next thing he remembers is his alarm going off and realising she didn't come home. That's when he started ringing around her friends and phoned the police to report her missing.

Hope would never walk out on her life. I just know something awful has happened to her. At this point, I'm not even sure he's called the police. I just don't trust him.

Glancing over at Hope's desk, I find myself looking at the photo of Fifi that appeared on her desk in a frame after the cat died. She took her death badly, taking a couple of days off afterwards. Now that I remember it, she told me how kind her neighbour Eileen had been. Eileen knows what Guy is like, has seen right through him according to Hope. Maybe I can contact Eileen to ask if she heard or saw anything.

Chapter Ten

Hope: Before

G uy Chambers is a beautiful man. Even when he is
angry, you can still appreciate his perfectly
proportioned face, his sensuous full-lipped mouth and deep
brown eyes. Meeting him for the very first time triggered a
physical response I hadn't felt before, a fizz of excitement
that was almost primeval. It seemed to elevate me to a
different level, and I know that I must have been radiating
pheromones like a bitch on heat. When Kylie arranged a
viewing for a townhouse in Warwick, I didn't know who
for, just that they wanted to view the property before work.
I collected the keys from the office the day before so that I
could go straight there from home the next morning.

Finding a parking space on that road during the morning
rush hour was a major hassle but I had no choice, as a
Porsche was parked in the allocated parking space. Walking
towards the house, my eyes fixed on a tall, dark-haired,
well-built figure loitering outside the front door. As I got
closer, he checked his watch. It wasn't a promising start.

"Hi, are you waiting to view the house?" I asked in my
professional voice—warm and friendly to put clients at
ease. He did something that looked like a double take, a sort
of perfunctory look followed quickly by a probing stare that
hit the mark inside me. I held out my hand. "Guy

Chambers?" I queried. His handshake left a dull ache in every bone of my hand, and I made a mental note not to let him dominate me like that again.

The house was set on three floors, with a large kitchen diner on the ground floor, leading off to the entrance hall and stairs. The owners had obviously spent a lot of money on the interior and furnishings: from the handmade Shaker kitchen to the parquet floor in the lounge on the first floor. The authentic Chinese rugs to the custom-made sofa and chairs that had clearly been designed to complement them perfectly.

On the top floor, there was an expensive mahogany sleigh bed in the master bedroom with its own deluxe en-suite. From the bedroom, you could access a roof terrace that was designed to provide maximum privacy with an impressive view of Warwick Castle. Everything was perfect. Even a man who drove a Porsche, for I was now sure it was his, would be happy with that house, and yet... he still managed to find faults. "The rooms are quite small." Yes, it's a modern townhouse. "The décor in the master bedroom isn't quite to my taste."

I felt myself suppressing a sigh until I turned from the bedroom window to look at him. He was staring at me appraisingly. His rich brown eyes sent a shiver down my spine.

I thought I saw a slight smile on his lips as he spoke. "I'll take it. I haven't seen anything better than this." His voice was precise, as if he were addressing a meeting. "I'll come to your office tomorrow to complete the paperwork."

As we left the property, he placed a hand on the small of my back. Just a fleeting touch to gauge my response. He turned to face me. "Would you have dinner with me one evening?"

My initial response was to politely decline, as I don't date clients, but given what I was feeling about my social life, or lack of it, and my curious attraction to that man, I found myself agreeing to dinner against my better judgement.

So, here I am, approaching the restaurant to meet him. I can hear a piano; a ballad I can't quite place. The restaurant is busy, and the dim lighting in the room makes it hard to spot Guy. Hesitating in the doorway to adjust my eyes, a waitress approaches, but before she can speak, he is at my side.

He takes my hand and leads me to a table. And there it is again, that fluttery feeling at his touch. He takes my coat and hands it to the waitress. I'm not used to a man being this attentive.

Settled at the table—a paint wash affair in pale cream, the grain of the wood still showing through—I look up to find him staring at me over the lit candle in the middle of the table.

"I wasn't entirely sure you would come, but I'm so glad you did." He tries to hold my gaze. The feeling of nervous excitement, if that's what it is, persists.

"I don't usually socialise with clients," I reply carefully.

"What made you change your mind?"

"I'm not sure. Maybe I'm searching for a certain vulnerability beneath that arrogant exterior."

He gives me a penetrating stare and then smiles and shrugs, unconcerned. I suspect he rather likes the image he portrays.

The wine is good: New Zealand Sauvignon Blanc. A sip of the cold clear liquid flows slowly through my body, and I begin to relax. He's a charming but challenging dinner companion.

He tells me he's a law graduate from the University of Bristol and has worked in London ever since. "Back in the day, once you finished a law degree, you had to do a further year at a law college before you were allowed to practice. I

went to Chester. I'll take you there for a long weekend."
His eyes are appraising me to see how I'm taking his bold
move.

"You're getting ahead of yourself again," I reply calmly,
taking another sip of my drink.

"We're not a pair of teenagers anymore, Hope, why drag
out the courting ritual? Sometimes, you need to just go for
it and see what happens."

I hold his gaze for a moment before looking away. "I'd
like to know a bit more about you first. You could be a
serial killer for all I know."

He laughs so loudly he attracts the attention of other
customers. "If I were, I would hardly be likely to tell you."

He tells me he married another lawyer in his early
thirties, but it only lasted a couple of years. She left him; he
was heartbroken. Deciding he didn't want to live in London
anymore, he relocated back to the Midlands, where he'd
grown up, after securing a job with what he described as "a
good firm".

"And that's how I met you." He gives me a wolfish grin,
which I'm sure is supposed to be attractive but actually
unsettles me.

I take another sip of wine to restore my equilibrium. I'm
not surprised or bothered that he's been married before. To
be honest, he originally struck me as a bit of a player, but as
the night's wearing on, I'm beginning to see a different side
to him. He seems to be actually quite vulnerable underneath
that showy, slightly aggressive exterior. Although I'm
attracted to him physically, I'm not sure I necessarily like
him as a person yet. There's just something that is slightly
off about him.

Despite my reservations, I agree to see him again for a
drink after work next week.

Chapter Eleven

Steven: Before

S ome people would say I've wasted my life, but I prefer to think of it in a different way.

I'm highly intelligent. And that's not me bragging or boasting or being full of self-regard.

But being this intelligent has a downside. Unless, of course, you have a charismatic personality to match your intelligence. Which I don't. In fact, I'm the other side of charismatic; I've been called tedious, tiresome, monotonous and wearisome but worst of all: repulsive. You see, not only am I not charismatic but I also have a few personality traits that might repel you.

Only one person ever thought anything of me; saw me for who I really am beneath the layers of oddness on show to the world. Sheltered by his love and care, I began to believe I was worthy of being loved. I'd always been an outsider, then I belonged to someone.

Until *she* came along.

When he left, it nearly broke me.

Now I've found him again, I can't let him go.

Chapter Twelve

Hope: Before

Wilde's Wine Bar is a popular place to meet after work. It's in the basement of what was once a Regency townhouse, now a shop, on the main Parade in Leamington. I arranged to meet him there, as it's convenient for me; just a short walk from our office and I feel on home turf there.

I take my time getting there, strolling from the office, browsing in shop windows, in the hope he'll get there first. I don't want to appear too eager and I hate sitting on my own with a drink, waiting for someone to arrive.

As I approach the steps down to the entrance, there's still a buzz of last-minute shoppers. I squeeze past a short, brown-haired guy in a shabby checked sports jacket and jeans. He smells vaguely of BO, which even the sweet smell from his vape can't hide.

"Excuse me."

He gives me a "fuck off" look but moves out the way anyway.

Guy, who is standing at the bar, looks over as I open the door. He waves in a slightly self-conscious way. A few people look like they're enjoying an afterwork drink in the cellar themed room, still dressed in their office attire. The main clientele—couples on romantic dates and groups of friends dressed up for a night out—won't arrive until later. I vaguely know the owner; he rented a house from us a few years ago. He's usually behind the bar, but today he's sitting at a table, working on his laptop. He catches my eye and winks as Guy carries a glass of house red for me and his Belgian pale ale to a table in the corner.

"Friend of yours?" he asks as he sets our drinks on the table.

"Yeah, I know him."

"Close friend?" He raises an eyebrow, watching me closely.

"None of your business," I say briskly, avoiding eye contact with him as we sit. Let him think what he likes.

He sits next to me at the table for four.

"So, what's your week been like?" He traces the back of my hand with his fingertips.

Snatching my hand away, leaning back from the table, I give him a hard stare. "Shall we start again?" This comes out sharper than I mean it to but I'm not quite sure of him yet. He's so cocky and sure of himself. He knows he's attractive and seems to think this gives him carte blanche. I'm not even sure if this is a proper date.

"I apologise," he says. "You look tense; I was trying to relax you." His deep brown eyes bore into me like a scolded puppy. My stomach does a little flip as I hold his stare.

"Let's just have a drink, a chat and see how it goes." I'm usually pretty honest with myself but I can't seem to admit his fingers stroking the back of my hand triggered something inside me.

I steer the conversation to his job, and we exchange anecdotes about work for a while.

"Are you in a rush to get home? Shall we eat here?" he asks once we finish our drinks.

"Sure. That would be nice."

"I need a loo break. I'll bring menus back with me."

I watch his retreating back, admiring his toned posterior encased in an expensive grey suit. Clearly, he goes to the gym. The suit jacket that matches the trousers is hanging on the back of his chair. I steal a glance at the label: Armani. He must have been earning big bucks in his last job. I can't imagine a firm in Warwick paying a salary that would fund that lifestyle.

He returns with menus, and I find myself admiring his muscled shoulders and biceps through the material of his shirt as we decide on food. I settle for spiced cauliflower steak, hummus, capers, oregano and pitta bread—I'm toying with becoming a vegetarian. Guy orders a T-bone. As the night wears on and we share a carafe of red wine, our conversation strays to relationships.

"I can't believe you're single," Guy says as he pours me another glass of wine.

"Why can't you believe it?" I reply playfully. "You're single, and I have no trouble believing that. Or is this just a corny chat-up line?"

"God, you're direct." The corners of his lips turn upwards. "It's an invitation for you to tell me your relationship history. I've shared mine with you."

"Why would I want to do that?"

He pulls his chair closer to mine, pressing his left leg against my right. His arm is already threaded through mine, holding my hand on the table. "Because I think we both need to know where we stand before we start a relationship."

"You're very sure of yourself."

"Come on, be honest, there's a huge sexual attraction between us. I'm going to take you to bed tonight. It's going to happen. We both know it."

It must be the effect of the wine because I'm looking into his eyes while formulating an answer when I feel myself leaning in for a kiss. Our lips touch briefly. His mouth is full-lipped, and his light beard gently tickles my face.

Keeping eye contact, he moves in again and kisses me softly but passionately before tracing the contours of my jawline and neck with his lips as he whispers in my ear, "Come on, I'm taking you back to my place."

He drives with one hand on the wheel and one hand on my knee. As his hand moves up my leg and under the hem of my skirt, a shiver travels right through my body. It's been a long time since a man's made me tremble with excitement and even longer since I've ached for someone to take me to bed.

Glancing over at Guy, his eyes firmly on the road, I can see a smile playing around his mouth. I'm sure he's imagining what's going to happen when we get back to his place. Just the thought of what could potentially be running through his mind is turning me on. The doubts I had about him are receding, but I don't know if this is just lust temporarily clouding my judgement.

Chapter Thirteen

Steven: Before

I t began gradually during my last year at school. I guess
people imagine it is something you're born with and
signs of the illness first appear during childhood. This is not
usually the case. It was never the case for me. There were
definitely no signs before that final year at school. I
achieved ten GCSEs all at grade A. I was, I hoped, heading
for the same result for my four A level subjects.
Afterwards, I planned to go to Oxford to study English.

That all changed in the January of my final year at
school. I began to notice the first signs that something was
wrong. I thought maybe the pressure of the exams was
getting to me.

I had just finished my mock A levels when I began to
feel how I can only describe as totally fatigued. From time
to time, I felt especially tired and lethargic but nothing like
that new feeling of total, utter mental and physical
exhaustion. In the past, I'd had good relationships with a
small number of friends at school and latterly a steady
girlfriend for about six months. I got on well with most of
my family, especially my father who was a friend and
companion as well as a parent. But I gradually began to
stop socialising with my friends—not because I did not

want to see them, I just couldn't summon the physical or mental energy to go out.

Every day was the same as I struggled to work up the mental process required to get me through the school day: my brain ached, my legs and arms felt sluggish and heavy, even swallowing was an effort. Everything was becoming a chore. I felt disinclined, for the first time ever, to go to school. Everything would be alright for an hour or so in the morning. I would feel normal, interested, and it was easy to assimilate and retain information. Then, gradually, as the day unfolded, a mist would start to descend. I would feel fuzzy-headed however hard I tried to concentrate. My attention would wander to something else. I'd begin to panic as I made silly, elementary mistakes which both annoyed and frustrated me. I just wanted to get away from school, to run away from everything and leave it all behind. I craved solitude.

By that time, my parents were concerned. Dad suggested I go and see a doctor. He thought I had maybe contracted a virus like glandular fever. I dutifully went to the doctor, who said there was nothing wrong with me physically. He told me I was probably just overworking myself and feeling the effects of stress.

I tried to accept that, but as the weeks progressed, I felt less and less inclined to go out until I was virtually living in my bedroom. I stopped having my meals with the family. I did not want to see or speak to anybody. I tried to carry on with my revision, as that seemed the only safe thing to hang on to. My dad was beside himself with worry. Hurt and frustrated that he could not "get through to me". He was trying to be compassionate and understanding. We both agreed that I should concentrate on getting through my exams and then we would try to sort things out afterwards. I think he believed that once the exams were over, everything would go back to normal. He kept saying all I needed was a long holiday. Quite frankly, that would have put too much stress onto me.

I managed to get to school to take the exams. Dad dropped me off in the morning and Mum picked me up in the afternoon. The sense of dread upon seeing the building was overpowering. The feeling that everyone was looking at me, laughing at me, talking about me behind my back. I got through, just, without cracking totally. A few of my old friends tried to pick back up where we left off. Guy was especially kind and sympathetic. He made a point of seeking me out throughout the day so that I was not alone. He tried to make conversation with me but did not press if I could only respond with words of one syllable. He would just stand beside me in companionable, supportive silence.

The results of my exams were poor for me. I passed them all. Just. By this time, I was past caring. Dad talked about re-sitting them once I was well again. He said I should still aim for university. We talked about having a year off first. I had, by now, almost totally lost contact with my friends. My family, saving Mum and Dad, had grown tired of my behaviour. I felt isolated. Most of the time, I did not care. I felt like I was barely hanging on to my sanity. It is difficult to describe the feelings I had to someone who has not suffered like that. If you can imagine what it would be like to have a brain which is slowly melting, you might be able to begin to understand what I went through.

On the rare occasions I felt optimistic about the future, I imagined that when I got better, I could make a fresh start with my life. I wanted to be normal; to fit in. It's so lonely being on the outside all the time.

Chapter Fourteen

Kate: After

E ileen is sitting in a seat by the window of the café when I arrive, so it's easy for me to spot her. Her silver-grey hair glints in the sun reflecting off the window. She wears it in a modern short style, cropped around her ears and fuller on top. Although I know she's in her mid-seventies, if I hadn't known, I would have assumed her to be at least ten years younger with her slim figure, chinos and Breton style top. I hope I look that good when I'm her age.

"Hi, Eileen, sorry that I'm a bit late," I say, taking the seat opposite her. "I had to take a phone call just as I was about to leave the office."

"It's no problem," she replies, holding her mug with two hands, taking another second to peer out the window. "I was just enjoying sitting here with my coffee, people watching."

"Would you like another coffee and something to eat?" I ask as I beckon the waitress over.

"I'll have another cappuccino." Her eyes dart to the chalkboard menu on the wall. "A slice of lemon drizzle would be nice as well, please."

We make polite small talk until our order arrives. I wasn't sure she was going to meet me, considering we've hardly spoken in the past, but she seemed quite willing when I knocked on her door this morning before work, asking if she'd meet me for lunch.

Once the waitress has set our things down, Eileen takes a sip of her fresh coffee.

"I don't suppose you've invited me here to discuss my garden and the weather, Kate." She sighs, placing her mug back on the table.

"No. No, Eileen, I haven't," I say hesitantly.

"You want to talk about Hope." It's a statement, not a question. And not a surprise, considering she knows Hope is missing and I'm Hope's closest friend.

"Yes, I do," I say, meeting her steady gaze across the table. "And about Guy. Or, more specifically, about anything you can tell me about their relationship leading up to Hope's disappearance."

Eileen stirs the cappuccino to get rid of some of the froth. "Well, I don't really know Guy. Guy always…" She pauses and licks her lips. "He always just seems uncomfortable with me, as if he'd rather be somewhere else than wasting his time making small talk with an old biddy like me."

"You're hardly an old biddy," I say, smiling.

"I scrub up well," she says, laughing. "But to him I'm older and maybe a bit too knowing, if you get my drift. I think he's worried Hope might have confided things to me."

"And did she?"

Eileen shakes her head. "Not really. We'd stop and exchange small talk if we passed each other in the street, and she'd often apologise to me, asking if I'd been disturbed by the shouting. You couldn't help but hear it, you know; Guy has a loud, deep voice."

I bite my bottom lip. "I can imagine. I've seen his temper first-hand. And from what I know, the arguing was getting more and more often. Did you ever hear what they were arguing about?"

"I couldn't hear the actual words. And it was mostly Guy I heard, not Hope. There was one occasion when it spilled out into the street." Eileen looked down at the table, as if she were reliving the moment in her mind. "I thought she was going to leave in her car. I thought she was *finally* going to walk away from him. In the end, she went back into the house with him." She paused and moved her eyes from the table to me. "I don't know why and I could be wrong but I have a feeling he might've been hitting her."

I break eye contact with Eileen and swallow.

"He was hitting her, wasn't he?" Eileen asked, staring at me hard.

"Yeah, I…" I shrug. "I mean, I know he did at least once."

Eileen tutted and stabbed her lemon drizzle aggressively with her fork. "I knew it. I just *knew* it."

"Mhm, she was a right mess when she came to work." I jab the table hard with my forefinger at each word as I say, "I've never trusted that man. There's always been something about him." I have to take a deep breath to compose myself and move myself back to what I need to find out. "Did you see or hear anything happen in the week before she left?"

"Not really. I'm sorry I can't be more helpful."

I nod. "I'm sorry to ask this, and you'll think it a really odd question…" I hesitate, playing with my teaspoon to give me time to word the question carefully.

"Go on," she prompts.

I take a deep breath. "Do you think Guy could have killed her? How has he been behaving since she disappeared?" A massive part of me thinks I've asked too heavy a question, considering Eileen is practically a stranger to me, but I'm at the point I don't care; I'm just desperate to find Hope. And although I hate to admit it,

Eileen may have heard more through those walls than Hope told me.

She tilts her head to one side. "I can't lie, that thought has crossed my mind." She takes another sip of her coffee. A faint line of froth lingers on her top lip. "He comes and goes from the house, presumably to work, but he hasn't spoken to me." Eileen leans over the table and covers my hand with hers. "I know you're worried about her. I am too. Such a lovely young woman and has been nothing but polite to me. But there is one thing I can tell you: a man has moved in with Guy. It might be his brother. He seems to be living there permanently."

I raise one eyebrow, struggling to work out who this strange man could be. "He doesn't have a brother."

"A friend, then. He must be keeping him company. It's strange though, I'm sure I've seen him before. It was a few months ago, during the day. They were both out. I just happened to be looking out of my front window when I saw him ring the doorbell. When he got no reply, he peered through the lounge window before walking away. I'm sure it was the same man."

Chapter Fifteen

Milly: After

Dan's loading the dishwasher after our evening meal. I'm standing in the kitchen with a glass of wine, watching him. He stacks the dishes in a really methodical way, as if he's still on manoeuvres in the army. My haphazard approach appals him. Apparently, I only ever manage half a load because of my inability to stack properly. The disagreements we've had over this have led to him always being the one to load the dishwasher, which suits me fine. In return, I do the laundry.

"What are you thinking about?" he asks quietly. "You seem to be in your own little world tonight." He closes the dishwasher door and switches it on before he turns towards me, concern all over his face. "What's the matter, Mills? Come here." He opens his arms to wrap me in a bear hug.

"That girl in the car."

"It's really got to you?"

"Yes, I can't stop thinking about her. Wondering if she is alright. I think I'll go to pieces if they find her body."

"It's not your fault. You did everything you could." He gently pushes my chin up until I'm looking directly into his kind blue eyes.

"I should have been braver and followed them straight into the house after I called the police. I'll have to live with that forever if they find her dead. I feel as if I've let her down in some way." I gently push him away so that I'm not distracted by the feel of his fingers massaging my back. "I should be doing something more now. I just don't know what." A slight note of hysteria is creeping into my voice.

"Stop beating yourself up. The police will be doing everything they can. Just because it's not in the news every day doesn't mean they aren't still actively looking for her. There will be a team working on it behind the scenes."

"I wish they would let me know what's going on." I start to nibble the skin around my thumbnail—a nervous habit I've had for as long as I can remember.

Dan gently encloses his hand around mine, taking it away from my face. With his free hand, he strokes my cheek. "You're making your thumb bleed. Would you feel any better if we retraced the journey from where you first saw her? See if we can jog your memory to remember anything else?"

Would this really help? I've seen re-enactments on *Crimewatch*, and I guess the police wouldn't do this if they didn't get results from it... I turn my face to kiss his fingers softly. "Would you really do that with me? I mean, I'd feel so much better if we could. I think it might help me. Even if it leads to nothing, I'll feel that I'm at least doing something."

"We'll go on Saturday. It'll give you something to focus on."

It's as if a weight has been lifted from my chest and I can just about breathe properly again. I smile, throwing my arms around his neck. "Thank you. I do love you. You're such a good person."

"So are you," he says, putting his arms around me and pulling me closer for a long, close cuddle. Resting my head on his chest, his woolly sweater tickling my nose, I think about how lucky I am to be here with him. And then my face drops, guilt seeping in. How can I be so happy and safe and comfortable while the woman in the car doesn't have this? She may at this very moment be being held captive somewhere without any hope of being found and here I am smiling and cuddling up to Dan.

"What did you say the woman's name is?" Dan asks.

"Hope something. Chambers, I think the police said. Apparently, her husband phoned them and reported her missing. The woman I saw in the car matches her description."

Despite the warmth from Dan's body, I shudder involuntarily at the thought of what might be happening to her.

"This is the roundabout where the car pulled alongside me."

It's Saturday, and Dan is driving his new racing green Mini Cooper, which I think he secretly believes makes him look as if he belongs in the motor racing world. I'm directing him back over the route I followed the Golf on that day. It's as if I'm watching a film of the journey in my mind, remembering every little detail I can. All the time, I can't get her terrified eyes out of my head.

Despite driving at a slow speed with Dan listening as I talk through every thought and observation I had on that awful journey, we arrive in Corby without me being able to add anything new to my initial memory of events. The street is quiet, just as it was that afternoon. Dan parks outside the house in a vacant parking space. There is no sign of the blue Golf, but I'm not sure I expected there to be anyway. We sit in silence for a while as I mull everything over in my head.

"Has this helped?" Dan asks, turning in his seat to face me. He takes my hand in his, gently squeezing my fingers as reassurance.

I scrunch my mouth to the side. "I think we need to talk to the woman across the road. The one the police spoke to when I was here." I pause to see how he is taking this. "What do you think?"

"I don't see that it would do any harm. What do you want to say to her?"

"I just want to ask if she's heard anything more than I have."

"Ok," he says, letting go of my hand. "Let's see if she's in."

Standing outside her front door, I wonder if this is such a good idea after all; I don't even know her name. Unlike the house opposite, her house is pristine outside with a wood-panelled door painted in a sage green colour to match the window frames. It gives the house an old-fashioned cottagey feel.

I ring the bell, and we wait for someone to answer. I can't hear any movement inside. Looking up at the front of the house, no one appears at any of the windows. I ring the bell again just in case they're in the bathroom or otherwise engaged. We wait a full five minutes, but no one comes to the door. With one last look around, we reluctantly get back into the car.

"Can we go to Leamington to see where she worked?" I ask Dan as he starts the engine. "I've got it written down somewhere. The police told me she was an estate agent." I begin rummaging in my bag for the scrap of paper I wrote it all down on.

"I'm not sure that's such a good idea."

"Please, Dan, humour me. I need to do this."

He gives me a long, hard look, then sighs as he puts the car into gear and starts to move off. A high-pitched beeping noise startles me.

"Put your seat belt on," Dan says, pointing to the metal buckle swinging loosely next to me. I reach around for the seat belt, and as I do, a movement at the upstairs window of the neighbour's house catches my eye.

"Slow down, Dan." I open the window, sticking my head out to see more clearly, just in case it was a shadow on the glass. Everything is still again.

"What's the matter?"

Drawing my head back into the car, I reply, "I'm sure I saw movement at the upstairs window."

"Probably just a trick of the light as the car moved off. Do you want to go back and check?" We've reached the end of the road now.

"No. Yes. I don't know. It's just, I'm *sure* I saw someone." I'm visualising the image, trying to make sense of it.

"Yes or no? Do you want to go back or not?"

"Oh, let's just go to Leamington. If she is in, she probably won't tell us anything anyway." I'm trying to keep my stress inside, but you can clearly hear the irritability in my voice.

We drive on, heading for Leamington. Lost in thought, I haven't spoken for a while when Dan's voice breaks the silence. "Perhaps she doesn't want to speak to you?"

"You *do* think I saw something then, and I'm not just being paranoid?"

"It's possible. She could have seen us approach and doesn't want to get involved or it could be something more sinister. Is that why you didn't want to go back? You were worried I might think you're becoming paranoid about this?"

"A bit. To be honest, I'm beginning to doubt myself." I start to nibble my thumb again, drawing blood. And then my head catches something he just said. "Wait... like what?"

He glances at me quizzically. "What do you mean, 'like what?'?"

"When you said, 'it could be something more sinister.'"

"I don't know. If you let your imagination run wild, there are a number of possible scenarios."

"Exactly what I've been thinking. So, you do agree with me that it's strange?"

"Milly, the whole thing is strange. I really think it's best to let the police pursue this. I know you feel in some way responsible but you're not. I thought retracing the journey might help you clarify things in your mind. You did everything you could at the time. You don't know what you might be poking your nose into. I don't want you to get into trouble with the police or put yourself in any danger. You did the best you could on that day. You didn't just pull over and phone the police. You tried to help her, but now it's time to let the police get on with their job. They know what they are doing."

"But what if she's being held somewhere?"

"If she is, the person or people responsible won't be happy to see you snooping around. It's admirable that you are so concerned but promise me you won't do anything without me. I really have a bad feeling about this, and I don't want you doing anything on your own."

The Regency town of Leamington Spa is a smaller version of Cheltenham—elegant and upmarket. As its name suggests, it was once a spa town. The main shopping area is on the Parade, the main road running through the heart of Leamington. I've been here a few times for lunch and shopping with a friend. It's the sort of town I'd love to live in one day. The perfect place for a town-loving dweller like me, with its wide boulevards, Regency buildings, cinema and two theatres right on your doorstep. There's also a lovely park, the Jephson Gardens and lots of cafés and restaurants. When I mentioned this to Dan, he mumbled something about winning the lottery or an inheritance, neither of which we have much chance of.

At the south end of the Parade is a service road called Euston Square, which is situated just behind a war memorial. This is where the majority of estate agents in the town are to be found.

Dan parks in a multi-storey car park beside the cinema, and we walk back towards the Parade, crossing the road to the war memorial and then walking the length of Euston Square to locate the lettings agency where Hope worked before she went missing. Her disappearance has merited a small piece in the national press which reported that she co-owns the agency with her friend and business partner, Kate Parkinson.

Standing outside the green and white facade of the building, I look in the window at the photographs and descriptions of properties to rent. I can just see into the office behind the property descriptions. A young girl with long blonde hair and glasses is sitting behind a desk, working at a computer. A tall, elegant woman with a well-cut, brown-highlighted bob, in a plain navy-blue dress appears at her side. She looks towards the window and catches my eye as I pretend to read the property details. She turns her attention back to the girl at the desk.

"Do you think that's Kate Parkinson?" I ask Dan.

"It could just be someone who works there. Why? You're not thinking of going in, are you?"

"I thought I might go in and introduce myself to Kate if she's there. Tell her how sorry I am that I couldn't do more to help and ask if she's heard anything more about the investigation."

"I don't think that's a good idea, Milly. She might find it intrusive."

But I've already made up my mind, pushing open the heavy glass door to the office. He follows me inside.

The young girl with glasses looks up from her computer. "Hi, can I help you?"

"Is Kate Parkinson in?"

"Yes, do you have an appointment with her?"

"No, but I wonder if I can have a word with her? It's personal."

"Can I ask your name?"

"I'm Milly Hall. Tell her it's to do with Hope Chambers."

The colour drains from the girl's face. "I'll... I'll s-see if she is available," she stutters. "Just wait here, please." She looks from Dan to me, unsure of our intentions.

She disappears into a room at the back of the main office. When she reappears, the tall, elegant woman with the bob is following her. We're the only people in the office, which makes it less awkward to broach the subject of Hope's disappearance.

"I'm Kate Parkinson. Can I help you?" she says, looking at me warily, her body language radiating tension.

"I'm sorry to bother you like this. I'm Milly Hall, the girl who saw Hope in the car and followed it to the house in Corby. I haven't heard anything from the police, and I can't stop thinking about Hope. I wondered if you've had any more news?"

Her tense demeanour relaxes a little, the strained look on her face replaced with the hint of tears in her large, kindly brown eyes. "No, I don't know what's happened to her or where she is." She regains control again. "There is nothing that I can tell you," she says, giving me a hard stare.

I must look crestfallen, as Dan puts his arm around me.

"Come on, Milly, let's go home. I think we are intruding here."

I shrug him off. "If you receive any news, will you let me know, please?"

Something seems to crumble inside her, her mouth trembling as if she is trying to control it and failing. "Sorry, I'm sorry." She wipes tears from her eyes with her fingers, smearing her eyeliner. "Please come into my office. Kylie, can you get us all a drink?" She turns to Dan and me, her eyes flitting between us. "Tea? Coffee?"

"Tea would be good for us. Thank you," I say, Dan nodding in agreement.

"Milk, no sugar for both of us," he adds.

Once in her office, we sit in the two chairs, more comfortable than they look, positioned opposite her desk, in the corner by a window overlooking the back of the building. Her desk has a pile of official looking documents —contracts maybe—and a computer. A family photograph of two grinning small children and a fresh-faced guy with dark hair standing in a sand dune with the sea in the background sits next to the computer screen. Across the room, another desk is at an angle to Kate's. It houses not much more than a computer and a photo of a well-fed tabby cat. A large white mug with two cats on it is crammed with pens and pencils. A laptop lies closed on the desk next to the computer.

"Hope's desk. Ready for when she comes back," Kate says as she catches me glancing over. She looks on the verge of tears again.

"I'm so sorry. It must be really hard for you coming in here each day and seeing her things waiting for her to come back."

Chapter Sixteen

Steven: Before

I 've lost interest in reading. Once a great passion of mine, now I can't concentrate. My mind wanders to anywhere else but the pages and the words.

"Why not use pills? Just take a hundred or so and go to sleep forever."

"Shut up," I growl through gritted teeth.

"Hanging is more difficult—how to get the rope, where to put it, will the frame be high enough? Then again, would a knife be easier? Get in the bath; run the water; two quick, deep slits; let the blood drain away into the water. Endless sleep. Easy."

There it is again—that genderless voice. A voice that's been living inside me for weeks, taunting me, providing me with ways to end my life. A voice that won't go away even at night when I toss and turn, thrash, throw the duvet to the floor and try to focus on owls occasionally hooting and the small bits of traffic outside.

"Shut the garage door, start the engine, breathe the fumes. Walk to the motorway bridge, climb the railings, jump off."

"NOT YET," I shout. "I need more time. Give me more time."

A different voice chimes up. One that I don't hear as often and seems to sit in the back of my head, letting voice number one do all the work. I don't mind this voice as much. At least it's not trying to shower me with a million different ways to end my life when it pipes up. *"Get up. Get up now. Go for a walk and don't turn back. Go on, run away. Now. Now. NOW!"*

The first voice speaks again. *"Well, what are you waiting for? What are you hoping for? Do it now."*

"I said not yet," I hiss back.

The voices disappear as my bedroom door opens and my father walks in. "Who are you talking to?"

"There are people here," I reply. "Go away. I *need* to talk to them."

"There is no one here, Steven, you must have been dreaming." He doesn't even bother looking around my room to check.

"No, I need to be alone with them. Just go away and leave me to it."

My father stares at me in that warning way parents often do to their children when they don't want to flip out just yet but will if you push them. "I will be in the kitchen having a coffee. I'm making you one, too. You've got five minutes to sort yourself out and come downstairs."

Over the next few weeks, I begin to hold conversations with the voices regularly. They often start up as I'm wandering around the house. Sometimes, they're funny and we laugh and laugh about things that my family say and do. My family are ignorant—not clever enough to hear the voices and appreciate their humour.

One day, I walked out of the house while my father was talking to me. The voices were telling me to get out and were laughing. I listened and ran off down the street, round the corner, over the road, horns blasting, people staring, voices shouting. Later, while I was resting in the park, sitting on the grass, propped up against a wall, my brother appeared. He said that everyone was looking for me and that I was to go home with him. I trailed home beside him, neither of us talking.

My parents are forcing me to see a doctor. A psychiatrist. Someone to talk to and help me, they say. This is my last day at home for a while, as apparently they are sending me to a psychiatric hospital "to get better".

Chapter Seventeen

Hope: Before

The first two months, Guy and I met at every opportunity. We had sex in the shower, on the kitchen table, on the stairs, in my office after everyone had gone home and even in a hotel room one night after pretending to be strangers. It was addictive, electric, exciting, and I had never felt so happy and alive.

Month three, the first glimmer of something darker made a fleeting appearance.

We were on our way to visit friends of mine who lived in the North East of England. I'd been there a few times before on my own. That Saturday we went together, I got slightly lost. As we approached the junction on the A1 where we needed to come off, I could see the flashing lights of a police vehicle that was blocking the slip road. Halfway up the slip road, a car lay overturned, another car half across the road in front of the overturned vehicle.

"Use the satnav to find another route unless you know another way," Guy said as we drove past the scene.

"I think we can come off at the next junction and head back," I replied with a confidence I didn't feel.

Twenty minutes later, pretty much completely lost, I said, "Sorry, but I think we need to do a U-turn and head back towards Durham."

"Don't you know the route?" he said curtly.

"Yes, of course. We must have missed the turning."

"Well, that's your fault; you're navigating." His voice was becoming increasingly shrill.

There was an awkward silence in the car as he pulled off the road and into a side street, swinging the car around aggressively in a U-turn to head back in the direction we had just come from. We continued in silence, my stomach tensing uncomfortably. As we approached the correct turning, my heart sank, seeing it was blocked by a police car, maybe because of the same accident we had witnessed before.

"For fuck's sake," he exploded.

Trying to remain calm, I got the road atlas out. "If we get back onto the A1, we can go via Chester-le-Street."

"Are you sure?" he said angrily, almost spitting the words out. "Give me the map. Why didn't you just set the bloody satnav up like I told you to? You always think you know best." He indicated to pull over into a layby.

"Stop getting so rattled. It's not my fault the road is closed."

He turned in his seat to face me, making me flinch as he shouted directly into my face, "I wish we never came to this godforsaken place."

I was so shocked at his outburst that for once I was lost for words. Why on earth was he getting so angry about such a trivial thing? Yes, it was frustrating but not a major catastrophe. After sitting in silence for a moment, I said quietly, "Do you want to go home?"

"Yes. Phone your friend and make an excuse; I've no desire to be here or to meet her." He was sitting rigidly with his hands on the steering wheel, staring out of the windscreen. His voice was strained, each word clipped as if he was barely controlling his anger.

I took a deep breath. I hadn't expected that response. I thought maybe he'd apologise for losing his temper and we'd carry on our way. "She is one of my closest friends," I whispered. I kept my voice as calm as I could manage. I didn't want this to escalate, and it felt like it was close to doing so.

"I'm the only friend you need. Phone her and tell her we are not coming," he said adamantly.

I shook my head. "Just calm down. You'll enjoy yourself when you get there."

"Just bloody well do as you're told," he growled. Despite him still looking straight ahead, I could see his eyebrows furrowing.

And so, we made the long journey back, me trying to figure out what had just happened as I messaged my friend, making an excuse. He didn't say anything, and I was damned if I was going to fill the awkwardness with words. I switched the radio on as a kind of comfort blanket for me. We continued like this until we reached my home.

I asked him to drop me outside my house. He made to get out of the car, but I cut him off. "Don't come in. I want to be alone."

I got my bag out of the boot, and he sped off, leaving me standing in the road, not even waiting to check I got in ok.

The next day, he was sitting in his car outside my house when I went out to get some milk from the corner shop. He opened his window when he saw me.

"Hope!" he called after me as I walked down the street. I kept my eyes on the pavement and walked on, pressing my lips tightly together. He left his car to follow. I picked up my pace until he was almost running after me. He grabbed my arm and spun me around.

"Hope, stop, please let me apologise."

"You are an arrogant little prick, a big baby and totally selfish. Go away and stop bothering me."

"I have no defence. I fucked up big time. I'm sorry. I can only say that I've had a bad week at work. Forgive me," he said, keeping hold of my upper arms so that I had to stay and listen. "I love you." His eyes tried to read mine for a reaction to his pleading.

I consider myself to be a mature, intelligent, self-possessed woman, so why did I fall for that old corny line when that is the very moment I should have thrown the rose-tinted specs away and kicked him out of my life forever? I was and am to bitterly regret it. That will forever be the moment I think of as the missed chance I had to escape him.

"I love you, too," I replied.

Chapter Eighteen

Steven: Before

I 've been home from the psychiatric hospital a few months now, but I have to attend a day centre to continue my drug treatment and receive counselling to help me learn to live with my illness. They also want me to try and integrate back into society.

While at the hospital, I was allocated a bed. A doctor sat with me and talked me through what was happening to me. Nothing penetrated. I felt far away. The voices were telling me to get away and laughing at me. I wanted to escape from them as much as the hospital itself.

I was put on a course of medication. After a week, I began to feel calmer, and the voices deserted me.

The doctor and I had lengthy discussions about my feelings, how to cope with them and the importance of staying on my medication. He wanted to have a nurse visit me at home to help with the drugs, but I said that I could manage it myself.

No one mentioned the word "schizophrenia" despite me pressing the staff to tell me what was wrong and bringing that word up more than once. I just wanted to understand what was wrong with me so that I could try to make a life for myself in whatever form that might take. After weeks of frustration about the lack of progress with a diagnosis, it was the doctor that finally confirmed my suspicion. Of course, it wasn't just about me. My parents were also having to come to terms with my illness. I suspect they were having counselling to help them cope. Maybe they're still having it.

I was allowed home at weekends. When this seemed to go well, I was finally discharged six weeks later. During this period, Guy would call at our house to see me when he was home from university. Aware of my situation, I'm sure he edited his conversation to make his life seem less interesting than it was. Still, the university life that he portrayed seemed unobtainable to me and it made for a hard listen. Once, when I was going through a stable period, he invited me to stay in Bristol for a weekend. I was keen to go and started planning the trip. My parents quietly phoned Guy and told him they were worried I might have another episode while I was away, and they thought it was too much responsibility for Guy to handle on his own. The idea was gently put to rest.

I feel as if I'm always in the way. Guy spends so much time away now that he's at university, going through countless women along with his studying, and when he does have time for me and makes that extra effort to include me in his busy schedule, my parents step in. It's just not fair.

Chapter Nineteen

Hope: Before

I hear a slight banging noise and sigh, putting my coffee on my desk. I move the sales figures paperwork I was just going through into a messy pile and make my way out of my office. There's a rather scruffy-looking guy trying to open the main door. I raise my eyebrow, wondering how he can't open the door, considering we're open for business and the latch is off. I walk over and open it for him.

"Sorry." The man's cheeks blush a slight red. "I'm not very co-ordinated today." His gaze remains on the floor as he speaks to me, unable or unwilling to make eye contact. His short dark hair is greying at the temples, with flecks of dandruff scattered throughout.

"That's ok, what can I do for you?"

"I'm looking to rent a flat. Nothing too expensive though," he adds.

You get a gut feeling when you've been doing this job as long as I have, and something is telling me things don't add up with this guy. Over the years, I've met hundreds of people from all walks of life, with a multitude of reasons for renting a property. Some are searching for just the right property and have usually done their research before they arrive at the office. Other people are new to the rental market and need you to take them by the hand and lead them through the whole process. Some are older people going through a marriage breakup. There are even those about to be made homeless. This man doesn't strike me as falling into any of the categories. He just seems a bit of a lost soul really.

I sit at Kylie's desk, proffering her spare seat to him.

After turning Kylie's computer screen on, I search for our cheapest rental properties and show him the screen with details for three that are on the market for four hundred and fifty pounds a month or less. All are basic one-bed or studio properties in the town, near the railway station.

"Have a look at these and tell me if any look ok for you. I have time to arrange a viewing for one today. Can I just take a few details for our records?" I've got his full attention now. A look of panic crosses his face.

"What sort of details?" he says quickly.

"Name, address, phone number, just that sort of thing."

He chews on his bottom lip. "Can I take time to think about it? I'll get back to you. I'm not entirely sure I'm interested in what you have to offer." While a normal excuse to give, after the shock on his face when I asked for his details, I'm not completely sure this is his real reason for going no further. I seem to have spooked him. Perhaps he's walking out on a relationship but hasn't told his partner yet?

"Yes, sure, give me a ring if you want to view anything," I say politely. But you will still have to give me your details first, I think.

As he approaches the door, I watch to make sure he can open it ok this time, ready to help if necessary. When the door closes behind him, I sit motionless for a minute, staring at the screen. A sense of sadness lingers behind him, and I find my thoughts returning to him long after he's gone. Against my better judgement, I even mentally match him with a property, but I know in my heart that he won't return.

I spend the rest of the day busy with contracts—we've had five handovers this week, which means a lot of legal paperwork to complete. At six o'clock, Kylie pops her head around my door to say she is off home.

"Can you lock the front door for me before you go?"

"No problem. I might be a bit late in tomorrow morning, as I've got a doctor's appointment. I might have to wait a bit. You know what it's like."

"That's ok. Kate will be in early tomorrow. She's doing a handover," I reply, sighing and grabbing another pen, as the one I'm using has run out of ink.

"See you," Kylie calls out as she heads past my office for the back door. I hear it slam shut as she leaves. I wish she would pull it to rather than letting it slam shut behind her. After telling her this one hundred times and her still letting it slam, it's a battle I know I've well and truly lost. And it's not a battle I can be bothered to start up again.

It's past seven o'clock by the time I finish. It's a bit eerie being alone in the office at this time of the evening. The subdued lighting in the main office is throwing shadows on the walls. Once or twice, I've looked away from my screen, thinking someone's in the office but, of course, it's only the shadow of someone walking along the pavement outside the main window.

I take my coffee mug to wash up in the kitchen. Out of the corner of my eye, I think I see someone watching me through the main office window. We have property details in the windows, so it's not unusual for people to look at our windows, but it seems as though this person is peering through the gaps, trying to see into the office. As I approach the window, the figure disappears. It's probably nothing, just someone browsing, but it makes me feel uneasy and very aware that I'm alone in the office.

I quickly tidy my desk and turn my computer off. I switch the alarm on as I leave by the back door exit to where my car is parked. Reversing out of my space, I glance back at the office before I put the car into drive. Everything is still and quiet. I pull off and turn left to pass the front of the office, expecting to see the night light on in the main office and reassure myself that no one is loitering outside. Everything is in order, so I drive away, towards home. But when I look again, glancing in my rear mirror, I could swear the lights are no longer on.

Chapter Twenty

Guy: After

Hope has been gone for three weeks now. The police told me the longer someone's missing, the less likely they are to be found alive. I'm not sure I believe this in Hope's case. Deep down, I feel she's left me and is playing a particularly cruel game by masquerading as a missing person. It's not exactly a secret that she was planning on leaving. I didn't think she had the guts, but clearly another woman has managed to get one up on me. I get moments where I wonder if I'm wrong and she has come to some harm either by her own hand or someone else's but the timing just seems too perfect for that.

I wish I could say I miss her, but I'd be lying. I like having my own space again. I like the freedom to see who I want when I want. I like being free from the feeling that she's disappointed with the marriage and it's somehow all my fault.

The physical attraction, so strong in the first year we met, has long gone. Maybe that's all there ever was between us. I want children but here I am again at the tail end of another marriage. Callous as it sounds, a feeling of pure hatred has been steadily growing inside me since she disappeared. How can she expose me to this kind of scrutiny and think she can get away with it? Part of me hopes something bad *has* befallen her so that I can be rid of her while still eliciting a degree of sympathy for myself.

It's a fluke really that alerted me to the possibility she's alive and well and living her life somewhere else; just one of those coincidences that happens every now and again.

Mike Dwyer, our criminal law partner, popped his head around my office door one morning at work. "Got time for a chat?"

Our paths don't cross very often. Criminal lawyers tend to be out of the office more often than the rest of us due to the nature of their work.

"Sure," I replied, thinking he was going to offer his sympathy and advice about the Hope situation.

"I was in Exeter for a trial three weeks ago."

"Interesting, was it?"

"Kind of, but that's not what I wanted to talk to you about. I always get the train if I can so that I can work while I'm travelling." He hesitated for a moment, uncharacteristically unsure of his words. "The thing is, I think I saw Hope at Exeter St David's on the Friday night when I was returning. I was in a rush to catch my train. The lift was out of order, so I had to take the stairs. She was coming up the stairs on the other side from me. I only caught a glimpse but I'm sure it was her. I went on holiday for two weeks after the trial ended. It wasn't until I heard your news when I returned to the office that I realised the significance of it. The thing is, I should report it to the police. So, I'm giving you a heads up before I do." He looked away from me. "Do you think there's a possibility she just up and left you, Guy?"

A little surge of adrenalin pumped through me; a scent of danger. My heart skipped a beat, and I wasn't sure if it was through hope or despair. "Are you sure it was her?"

"As sure as I can be, which is pretty sure." He was watching me carefully, waiting for an answer to his question. I had to be careful what I said now. Mike was shit hot at eliciting the truth from someone—he had to be, that was his job.

"The truth is, I don't know. We haven't been getting on that well. I just want to know what's happened to her or where she is."

"Did you do something to her that made her leave?"

The question caught me off guard, and I furrowed my brows. "No, of course I didn't." I sounded aggressive and seriously pissed off, even to myself. But that was good, he would expect me to react that way.

"Calm down. I have to ask. You know that. You would do the same yourself."

"I never touched her," I reiterated forcibly.

Mike raised his eyebrows at me, narrowing his eyes, which bore into me like a proton beam. I don't think he believed me.

It's been barely a week since talking to Mike Dwyer. I return home from work to find Steven on my doorstep, his suitcase next to him.

Steven looks at the ground and bites the inside of his cheek. "I need somewhere to stay. Just for a few weeks at most, I promise."

I huff. Typical Steven—this isn't the first time he's annoyed a landlord. This also isn't the first time he's come to me for help. But now Hope isn't around... "You can stay with me for a while. Just until you get yourself sorted out."

He grins and follows me inside, wheeling his suitcase behind him. I wonder what I'll say if any neighbours enquire about him. I guess I can always say he's supporting me; there's always some nosy parker who wants to know all the ins and outs in your life.

After unpacking his suitcase, Steven comes downstairs and opens the back door. He lights a cigarette and looks out to the garden. I frown. I never allow smoking in the house, and he knows this.

"A colleague of mine thinks he saw Hope in Exeter the day after she disappeared," I say, trying to ignore the smell of the smoke.

Always a nervous sort of person, I watch his anxiety level go through the roof, his hands shaking as he tries to stub out his cigarette. "She can't be in Exeter. It's not possible." There's a rising note of panic in his voice as he turns back into the house and shuts the kitchen door with force.

"Well, it appears she is. I trust Mike Dwyer's observation skills. If he says he saw her, then he saw her."

"It's not possible," he says again, more emphatically this time. He starts searching for his cigarettes under the pile of junk he's left on my dining room table.

"Don't light that in here," I say sternly.

"But I need one." His hands are shaking as he flicks his lighter, completely going against my own rule in my own house. He draws hard, inhaling the smoke deeply, exhaling through his nose.

"She can't be in Exeter," he says again, quieter this time, almost as if it's only to himself.

"I need a drink." I pick up the bottle of Merlot I opened last night and left sitting on the table. The unwashed wine glass is still there too. What a slob I'm becoming since Hope left. Taking a large swig, I turn back to Steven, who is inhaling so deeply his lungs might explode. I can't seem to summon the mental energy to get him to put it out.

"What should I do now?" I ask, staring into the bottle at what remains of my Merlot. Exhausted after all the drama of the last few weeks, I just want to block it all out for a while.

Moving over to get closer to me, Steven puts his arms around my waist and leans his head on my chest. I put the bottle down so that I can put my arms around him. He's silently crying, the front of my shirt getting damp with his tears. A gut feeling, call it intuition if you want, signals an alarm.

"What have you done?" I say softly.

"Nothing." His reply is muffled as he buries his head into my chest. We stay like this for a while, comforting each other. But I'm not sure I believe his denial.

I'll have to employ a private investigator, a friend of mine who's worked for me before on a litigation case. If Hope is in Exeter, he will find her.

Chapter Twenty-One

Hope: After

I put my left hand against the door of the café, pushing it open and feeling the warmth flow over me. I glance around the room, hoping my favourite table is free. It is. I give a little wave towards Jenny at the counter as she makes a coffee for a customer. The sound of the coffee machine hissing in the background follows me to my seat by the window. Pulling the wooden chair out from under the table, I sit with my back to the brick wall, looking out of the window, up Market Road. Jenny has had a painting session and the once plain pine chairs are now a shade between pale green and duck egg blue.

I wait for her customer to move away from the counter before I approach, leaving my coat on the back of the chair. "Hi, Jenny, have you got any cheese scones left? I'll have a coffee with milk as well, please."

"I've put one aside for you. Do you want it warmed up?"

"Thanks, that would be nice. The wind's bitterly cold today."

She makes my coffee and hands it over to me with a little homemade biscuit. "I'll bring the scone over when it's ready."

I make my way back to my seat as another customer enters the café, letting a gust of chilly wind into the room.

Wrapping my hands around my coffee mug, the warmth spreads back through my body as I stare out of the window. In the background, I can hear the customer asking Jenny for an Americano. He's not from around here; his public-school accent contrasts with Jenny's soft Devon burr. Sipping my coffee, mentally miles away from here, the conversation recedes.

"Here's your scone." Jenny appears at my side. "How are you settling in?"

"Very well actually. I'm really liking it around here."

"Glad to hear. Just let me know if you need any help."

It's been two weeks since I arrived in Tavistock, seeking refuge with my old university friend. Phil had been a friend first and boyfriend later, and although we drifted apart after university, we kept in touch through the occasional text messages and emails. He never married, seemingly content on his own. It was in desperation that I asked him if I could stay for a few days.

He didn't ask any questions when I turned up on his doorstep with my suitcase. Instead, he welcomed me into his home and listened carefully when I told him the reason I was there. He offered me his spare room until I got myself sorted out, but I couldn't do that to him. Guy can be cruel and vengeful. I'd turned up on Phil's doorstep uninvited, asking for his help; I wasn't going to repay his kindness by putting him in the firing line. Besides, if Guy thinks I'm living with another man, I'll never see a penny of my money again. He'll make sure of that.

Phil helped me find somewhere to live, taking the lease out in his own name to protect my anonymity. It felt like old times again, transported back all those years ago to when life had been so much simpler. I just wish I'd realised that at the time. Wouldn't it be better if you could live your life backwards using all that information you garnered with age to make the right life decisions?

Feeling a bit emotional, I search for a tissue in my overstuffed tote bag and find the local paper I bought on my way to the café. My scone crumbles as I cut it in half, ready for me to eat. Flicking through the pages of the paper, I'm sidetracked by a photo of a young woman with a headline suggesting domestic violence is not always physical. The opening line of the article brings a fresh wave of tears to my eyes: *Is it possible to simply walk away from one life and start again?*

I blink the tears away as I try to focus on the words, taking a large mouthful of coffee to dispel the aching in my throat.

My instinct was to get as far away as possible from Guy. I hadn't really thought beyond that. I realise now that I was traumatised and in a state of deep shock. I just needed to get away to somewhere where I would feel safe. But now what? I suppose I have a vague idea that I will have to go back at some point to sort everything out. Sitting here in this café, away from everything, I can't think of anything I want more than to draw a line under the car crash that is my old life and start again. Is that possible? I'll have to sort things out with Kate but otherwise what is there to go back for?

I take another sip of coffee as the idea starts to take hold. For the first time in years, I feel a little glow of happiness begin to grow inside me. Maybe, just maybe it might work…

Chapter Twenty-Two

Milly: After

"I'm not sure I should be talking to you," Kate says.

Blonde-haired, smiley Kylie brings three mugs of tea on a tray and quietly sets them down on Kate's desk. "Is there anything else I can do for any of you?" she asks, looking around with a forced smile.

"Thanks, Kylie, everything is fine here." A look passes between them that tells me Kylie won't be leaving the premises while we're in the building. Nevertheless, Kate gives her a reassuring smile as Kylie closes the door.

"I understand you might feel uncomfortable talking to us," Dan says. "You don't really know that we are who we say we are."

"No, I don't," Kate replies, her fingers nervously playing with the edges of a contract on her desk. She takes her mug from her desk and cradles it in her hands as she sits back in her chair.

"Would you like to call the police to verify who we are?" Dan asks.

"Do you have any ID?"

We both get out our driving licences and hand them over.

"Thank you." She writes down our details, including our address, on a pad. I guess for her to check out later with the police. Then, she looks up, her eyes piercing right through me. "Now, tell me from the very beginning exactly what happened that day."

A week later, now the beginning of October, I find myself sitting in the same seat. This time, Kate invited *me* to meet with her. I've come straight from work, and her office is closed, Kylie already home so we won't be disturbed. I guess she's checked me out with the police because she's so much more relaxed and friendly this time. I observe her through the open door as she makes coffee in the kitchen at the back of the office. Tall, about five foot ten to my five foot four, slim but not skinny. There are dark circles framing her eyes despite a layer of concealer that does nothing but sink into the tired lines, accentuating them more.

"I'm sorry that I was a bit off with you last week; I thought you might be the local press."

I get up and join her in the kitchen. "Not a problem. If I'd been in your position, I would have felt the same way. It probably wasn't very sensible of me to turn up like that without phoning you first."

She finishes making the coffee and hands me a large mug filled to the brim. "It's just that Kylie and I have been approached for an interview on several occasions. One guy even turned up at the office pretending to be a client."

I sip at my coffee, feeling the scalding liquid burn the back of my throat. I follow her out of the kitchen, trying hard not to let the coffee spill onto my hand.

Back in her office, she passes a box of biscuits over to me. "You must be hungry if you've come straight from work."

I opt for a plain digestive despite being tempted by the chocolate biscuits. In some strange way, I feel I have to impress Kate in order to be taken seriously by her, and plain feels like a "mature" option. Not that she takes any notice as she sits at her desk, staring into space.

"I just want to help in any way I can. I sort of feel responsible." Kate turns to blankly look at me, not quite understanding. I continue, "If I'd phoned the police straight away, she might've been here now. It was just instinctive to follow the car. I don't have handsfree."

"How much do you know?"

"Nothing," I reply. "The police won't tell me anything."

"The police are treating Hope as a missing person, as there is no evidence any harm has come to her. Her debit card was used at Corby station the day after she disappeared. She bought a ticket to London St Pancras. The station staff can't remember seeing her and neither can anyone on the train whom the police have been able to contact."

"It could be someone else using her card?"

"Yes, it could." She shrugs. "We just don't know." Her lips quiver slightly, and I think she's about to cry but then she takes a sip of her coffee to steady herself. "I just know she wouldn't have walked out of her life without telling me what was going on unless something dreadful has happened, preventing her from contacting me." She takes a deep breath to stem the unshed tears.

"This is our shared business," she says, indicating everything surrounding us in the office. "We've worked so hard to make it a success. She wouldn't just walk away. Where would she go? She hasn't used her debit or credit cards since. It doesn't make sense." She pauses, trying to compose herself, her mouth trembling slightly again. She takes a deep breath before continuing.

"The thing is, she wasn't happy before she disappeared. She was in what I'd class an abusive relationship. She talked about leaving her husband. The police, most likely prompted by him, think she's left home of her own accord, in a frail mental state, after a domestic incident and will reappear again at some stage. Guy, her husband, has an alibi for the day she disappeared. He was at work. The house you saw her in does have traces of her DNA but that's not surprising, as she showed someone around earlier in the day."

She stops talking, letting her eyes wander over to Hope's desk, the closed laptop sitting forlornly on top of the desk, waiting for its owner to return. She has a wistful look in her eyes, as if she can see Hope sitting there.

She turns her attention back to me. "I have to be careful what I say about her husband, as he's a solicitor. I tried to talk to him about Hope's state of mind the day she disappeared. I wasn't insinuating anything, but I guess that's how it came across to him. He told me if I badmouth him, he'll sue me for defamation of character. Let's just say her husband is a difficult character." She hesitates before continuing. I can see this conversation is very difficult for her.

"No one else knows this but Hope has the opportunity of setting up her own business in Northampton. She thinks it's an area that has development opportunities both as a commuter area for London and an area of growing employment opportunities. She was going to leave her husband and make a fresh start with her own business. Jamie, my husband, and I are in the process of buying her out of the partnership. So, you see, none of this makes sense. Something must have happened to her."

I nod as I exhale slowly, not sure how to take the news of Hope's difficult homelife. The more I know of her, the more I connect with the lady in the car as she's shaped into a real human and not just a facial glimpse. "I know it was Hope in the car. I've identified her from a photograph. She definitely wasn't in that car of her own accord. I can't just wait around and do nothing. I'm here for whatever help you need."

"I want to put an appeal out in the local press in Northampton and Corby to see if seeing her face jogs anyone's memory. The police have agreed to it. I've thought a lot about it since you contacted me and I think it will have more impact if you make a personal appeal for information, as you were the last person to see her. Will you agree to being interviewed by the press and local radio if necessary?" Kate looks directly at me, her eyes pleading for me to agree. "I know it's a lot to ask of you."

"Of course. I'll do anything I can to help," I reply.

Chapter Twenty-Three

Steven: The Happening

The sound of her breathing is really beginning to annoy me. It isn't just the ragged breathing as she threatens to break into tears, but the constant little sniffs that punctuate her breaths. I glance briefly at her sitting beside me as I drive. I find it hard to relate to the feelings of love and desire Guy said overwhelmed him when he first met her.

In my rear-view mirror, I can see the red Peugeot I pulled up sharply beside at the roundabout. My driving has never been great, and when I'm unwell or agitated, my driving can be very erratic. The car is probably just going the same way, but I better keep an eye on it just in case. Probably nothing. All the same, I don't want any complications at this stage.

"Where are we going?" Her tearful little voice breaks through my thoughts.

"You don't need to know. Stop snivelling, or I'll stop the car and hit you again. It's really getting on my nerves."

"My office knows where I am. If I don't return soon, they'll call the police."

"Is that a threat? It better not be. You don't seem to realise how precarious your position is."

Silence.

I glance in the mirror again. The red car is still in view but three or four cars behind now. I relax a little.

A movement from the corner of my eye brings my attention back to Hope; she's slowly trying to open the passenger door.

"It's locked," I say roughly.

She looks at me, her big blue eyes now red and swollen. Any traces of eye makeup have long since been wiped away with the paper tissue squashed in her hand. Her foundation patchy over her flushed cheeks. The anguish in her face makes my heart sing. I have played a secondary role to her and all the others who came before. Now, she will know how it feels to have her life taken from her; to be the person who has no control.

As I pull up outside the house, she gasps. "What are we doing here?"

"Just get out the car and walk to the front door. No funny tricks."

"I've just rented this house out." Despite trying to keep her voice calm, I can sense the rising hysteria bubbling away within her.

"I know."

She strives hard to control her mouth as her lips tremble. Just as she looks like she's going to start screaming, her face sags into a picture of misery as I reveal the gun hidden in my coat pocket.

"Don't try anything. I'm going to come around and help you out of the car."

As she gets out, she stumbles, falling into me. My inclination is to flinch from the feel of her body against mine but she's shaking so much that I have to link my arm through hers to get her up the path, the gun pressing firmly against her stomach. Hurrying her along the path, I fumble for the keys with my spare hand. Eventually opening the front door, I bundle her into the house. She turns her head for one last desperate look at the outside world before I shut the door firmly behind us, the sound of the key turning in the lock echoing through the silent house.

Chapter Twenty-Four

Hope: After

Phil's always been a calm, laid-back sort of person, so it's a surprise to see him so agitated. He's been irritable ever since he arrived at the cottage, snapping at me every time I try to engage him in conversation.

"Aren't you ready yet? I thought we were going for a walk," he says as I open the door.

"You're a bit early. Anyway, I thought we could have a coffee before we go."

As I usher him inside, he says brusquely, "I haven't got time for that; I've a hundred and one things to do today. We can't all just swan around, you know." I can't help but feel stung by his words.

"Maybe I can help you? We don't have to go for a walk today. I'll make a coffee and you can tell me all about it," I say, attempting to placate him.

"You can't help me."

"What's the matter, Phil?" I snap.

Grabbing my arm, he forces me to look at him. I guess he's been steeling himself to ask me something. In the end, he blurts it out.

"Are you pregnant?" he demands.

"Wh-why do you—"

"Every time you go to the café, you want a cheese scone. You *hate* scones. At least, you did before. And now you're eating them on the daily, you eat them at the café, you've got about five packs in the cupboard. So, unless I'm missing the point, those are some hefty cravings. Maybe I'm wrong, but… maybe there's a reason why you walked away from Guy when you did. Am I wrong?"

I take a deep breath. "I'm about four months gone."

The sun glints off the remains of the snow that's been ploughed to the sides of the road and the smattering sprawled across the landscape.

We walk in silence for a few minutes while Phil digests the information.

"You need to register with a doctor and plan for the birth," Phil states. "Does Guy know you're pregnant?" Phil's tone is deceptively calm. His mouth is set into a grim line, his head staring at the ground in front of him as we walk on. I can't tell if he's angry or hurt. Maybe it's both.

"There's plenty of time to plan for the birth. I'm fit and healthy. I can even deliver it myself if needs be. I've been watching YouTube videos to see what I have to do. I think I'll be able to cope." I study his profile as he walks, woolly hat pulled low so only his face is peering out. His breath forms little clouds in the cold air as he labours up the hill. My lovely friend, why didn't I marry you?

"And no, Guy doesn't know," I continue. "If he finds out, he'll track me down and have the baby removed from me when it's born. He's always wanted a child. He won't let this one go. I know him; he won't give up until he has denigrated my character enough for him to apply for full custody." As I'm saying this, the realisation of my words sink in, and a surge of panic sweeps through me.

"He can't do that," Phil says, shaking his head. "There are laws to protect you. I'm not saying it won't be hard, you'll have to fight your corner and withstand all the mudslinging, but I'll stand by you and so, I would imagine, will Kate."

"You don't understand; he's a solicitor. He knows how to play the system and he has free advice whenever he needs it. He's already tried to convince me I've got mental health problems stemming from childhood. I wouldn't stand a chance, Phil." The words are tumbling out of my mouth.

"You can't deliver a baby on your own. I won't let you. You need medical help." He still won't look at me. I'm beginning to sense disapproval, which unnerves me. He's my only friend now. If he turns against me, I don't know what I will do.

"We'll just see how it goes." I know I will do what I have to do but I don't want to fight.

"Why don't we go to the police? You were abducted, held against your will, left to rot in that place. The police *will* listen to you." He steps in front of me, facing me. "You've been reported missing, you know? We need to go to the police, Hope." His voice is gentler, as if he knows how close to the edge I'm getting.

"I know." I bite my lip. "I just can't have this child taken away from me," I say. "It's the most wonderful thing that's ever happened to me. I know in my heart it was Guy who tried to get rid of me but I have no evidence. I need to stay here until I feel strong enough to face the world again. Please, just give me time to do this."

Phil links his arm through mine reassuringly, and we walk on. I snuggle closer to him, squeezing his arm to say thank you. A few minutes later, we arrive back outside the cottage.

"Are you coming in, or do you have to get off?" I ask.

"One coffee will be fine."

We step inside and take our coats off. I put the radio on as the kettle boils. Phil's sitting at the table, scrolling through his phone. Suddenly, he stops, finger hovering over the screen, mouth opening.

"Hope, have you seen this? There is an appeal in the Northampton press for information about you."

"What? Let me see." I rush over and grab the phone from Phil's hand, quickly scanning the news article on the screen. It feels so strange to see my own face staring back.

"I've been keeping an eye on the local news for Northamptonshire and Warwickshire just in case the police started taking your disappearance more seriously. I just knew someone would be looking for you, Hope. It's best to know what is happening so you can plan what you need to do."

I pass the phone back to him. "It must have been Guy."

"No actually." He scrolls back to the top of the appeal and points at the screen. "Says here Kate Parkinson and someone called Milly Hall. She's the girl who saw you in the car apparently."

"Milly Hall," I mouth. Her small, startled face is etched deeply into my memory. She won't know what a comfort it was to see her car in the wing mirror, following us that day. It gave me the courage to do what I did.

If it weren't for her, I would be dead now.

"I need to get a message to Kate. Guy can't find out though."

Chapter Twenty-Five

Guy: After

Steven reacted badly to the news Hope had been seen in the Exeter area. I thought he would be pleased, as it would take some of the heat off me. I know the police are observing me as a person of interest. Why wouldn't they be? After all, this is the second time a wife has walked out on me, and it's well known the husband is always the number one suspect in any investigation into a wife's disappearance.

Steven and I have never lived under the same roof before. It feels strange and a bit claustrophobic. We met at school. There, he wasn't the most popular kid. He was clever and shy. I liked talking to him, though. He knew things about the world that I could never have known. He was like a walking encyclopaedia. It became a joke: ask Steven, he knows the answer to everything.

That's how he came to hang out with us, and we protected him from the bullies who would have eaten him alive otherwise. No one ever chose him for sports teams. My game was rugby. When yet another game rolled by and he was once again going to be the last to be picked for a team, I decided to help him by picking him before it came to that. I was the captain for this game, with two more players to pick. There he was, standing in his kit, weedy legs, weedy arms, blinking as if a speck of dust were caught behind his contact lens or something.

"Steven."

My team nearly choked when I said his name.

"Come on, Guy."

"Fuck it, Guy."

"Anyone but him."

"We've already lost the game!"

"Stop whinging. He might be our secret weapon." I nodded my head in Steven's direction to join the team. He looked grateful but terrified. I spent the whole game trying to protect him, but he was a quick runner, like a whippet, and proved quite useful to us in future games.

During breaktimes, I would make sure he was part of our gang. I couldn't bear to see him standing on his own in the corner of the playground.

When we left school, he came to see me at uni. We became friends, and then we became lovers. It was a casual relationship to start with. I was experimenting. Males and females. I knew I wasn't gay but sleeping with guys still appealed to me.

I had loads of girlfriends, liaisons, flings and one-night stands during my time at uni. It wasn't until I met Erica that I fell in love. When she left me, Steven was there to console me.

We weren't open about it, even to each other, but we did have real, more than just friends feelings. Whenever I was near him, I had to fight the urge to put my arms around him, stroke his hair, touch his mouth. I never asked him what he did when I wasn't around. I just assumed he was the same as me—playing the field with both men and women. I was wrong. He told me one night that he'd had a few relationships, but they always came to nothing, as none of them matched up to me. "I truly love you, Guy," he said. Maybe I loved him, too? I've always found that love is a multi-layered feeling with many colours. It can't be boxed up neatly and tied with a bow. For now, I have other reasons to protect him. It's a case of self-preservation for me. A lot depends on what I do now.

My mobile, on silent, flickers into life while I'm in a work meeting. I discretely check the message under the table. It's from Steven: **I've found her. She's living near Tavistock.**

At least I know she's still alive and presumably not injured in any way, otherwise how could she have found her way to Tavistock on a train? But why hasn't she contacted me? What if she's had a breakdown? Will I have to take her back and look after her?

"Do you think you can give us your full attention, Guy?" The senior partner glares at me.

"Sorry, Nick, I've been waiting for a call." I turn my attention back to the meeting. I can't think about this now. I need a clear head without any distractions.

Mike Dwyer smiles wryly at me from his seat further down the table.

Chapter Twenty-Six

Kate: After

"Look at me, Mummy," Chloe shouts from the shallow end of the pool. Jamie's holding her arms and pulling her through the water as her little legs splash about behind her. As she passes the end of the pool where I'm sitting in the viewing area with Oliver, who's asleep in his pushchair, she laughs. "I'm swimming!"

I wave at her as she goes by. There's a lot of joyful screaming and shouting from the children in the pool. Dads and mums with small children learning to swim. Some, like me, are just watching and supporting. I've been bringing Chloe here for over a year now. The pool belongs to a private school but is open to the public on certain days to teach younger children to swim. Chloe was struggling to learn even though we had been taking her to the pool at the gym Jamie goes to. She was petrified of the water. One of the other mums suggested I bring her here. It's worth the expense. Chloe has gained a lot in confidence from the one-to-one tuition. She can finally swim and even enjoys going to the group sessions, like this one, which she hated before.

Scrolling through my phone to kill time, I click onto WhatsApp as a message pops up. It's an unknown number. No photo: **Please don't look for me. I'm safe where I am. The police know I'm safe now. Sorry for everything.**

My mind goes blank. The echoes of the children's voices bounce off the roof of the indoor pool while I remain frozen, staring at my phone.

Hope's still alive.

My brain can't quite comprehend it yet. I'm feeling a muted sort of euphoria. She's alive and living her life somewhere out there. Somewhere that I'm not a part of. I'm happy and sad and confused and maybe a little hurt. Why didn't she reach out to me?

"I need to talk to you," I say to Jamie as he walks down the stairs after tucking the kids in bed.

"Yeah, sure, what's up?" He walks to the front room and sits on the sofa, staring at me expectantly.

"It's about Hope. She's alive." I can't stop grinning as I tell him.

Jamie's face is a picture I can't quite work out how to decipher. Happy? No. Shocked? Yes. Disappointed? Maybe. I hope I'm wrong about my last thought.

"So, he hasn't killed her."

I can't deny that the thought has been at the forefront of my mind as the days have dragged by, but for some reason, he seems less than happy about the situation, as if part of him wanted to be proved right that Guy was capable of such an act.

"Did you think he had?" I reply.

"In all honesty… yes. Either by design or by accident. We both know I can't stand him. You can't either. There's a reason neither of us like him. I wouldn't put anything past that man."

"Something awful must have happened to make her run away like that. What I can't understand is why she didn't come to us. It's not like we wouldn't have helped."

"Maybe she didn't want to cause trouble between us?" Jamie shrugs. "Uh, for us, I mean."

"Why would she cause trouble for us?" I look at him, puzzled, a nasty little niggle burrowing away inside me. "I thought you liked Hope?"

"Yeah, she's fine. She's your friend, and we get along." There's something about the way he isn't quite looking at me, squirming in his seat as if he can't get comfortable. I can't work it out. His comment makes even less sense to me now he's confirmed they get along. Unless he doesn't actually like her, or they've had a clash I don't know about? Maybe they just pretend to like each other for my sake.

"What did the police say?" he says, dragging my attention back from the puzzle he'd created in my mind.

"They thanked me for contacting them, said they've been in touch with the 'missing person' but that they can't give me any more details."

"So, what do we do now?"

"I guess we carry on as normal until she contacts me again; respect her privacy. I can't see what else we can do." How I feel is a stark contrast to the calm and rational speech coming out of my mouth. I know that some appalling incident must have occurred to make Hope run away from her life and effectively go into hiding. Deep down, I'm also more than a little hurt and upset that Hope didn't come to me for help and that it took her so long to contact me. But I have to push these self-centred feelings away. There must be information I don't yet know.

Despite her still not having opened my earlier text I sent while at the swimming pool, I send her another asking her to contact me as soon as she can and telling her I love her. I also tell her she's welcome to stay with us when she's ready to come back and that if she needs me, I will come to her wherever she is. I try phoning but the line is unobtainable, so I don't know if it's even possible for her to read my texts.

Chapter Twenty-Seven

Hope: After

Although I went to Devon for holidays as a child, we always stayed in the seaside resorts of Torquay, Brixham and Woolacombe Bay. We never ventured into the countryside and towns around Dartmoor, so Tavistock was a revelation to me. A tourist brochure would describe it as a lovely ancient market town tucked away on the edge of Dartmoor. I first dared to venture into the town a few days after I arrived at the cottage. I felt like a little mouse emerging from its burrow at the end of a long winter, sniffing the air to see if it was safe to come out. For someone who'd always been so confident and independent, I felt tiny, curled into a ball inside myself, frightened to unfurl and face the outside world.

No longer sure of my place in the world, I'm trying to come to terms with feeling bruised both mentally and physically. The deep grooves in my wrists and ankles are already beginning to heal but no lotions or drugs can help with the emotional wounds.

Stepping off the bus, into the bustling main street in Tavistock with its independent shops, Pannier Market, cafés (including Phil's), restaurants and hotels always makes me feel as if I'm traveling from the moon to the centre of Oxford Street. There is a thriving vibe about this place. In another life, I would relish living here. I can see myself buying a home, opening an agency and settling here for the rest of my life. Back in the real world, I'm living a reclusive life on Dartmoor with occasional visits to the town to keep me sane and to buy essentials.

It's been three weeks now. I'm beginning to recover from the shock. I've stopped sleeping for fifteen hours a day and sitting alone at the cottage, rocking myself backwards and forwards while reliving every minute of that day and night.

Phil helped me through the police ordeal; I couldn't find the right words to explain what happened. Part of me wanted to blurt out that I thought my husband had arranged for me to be killed but the words wouldn't come out. A primordial fear that Guy would destroy me emotionally if I tried to bring him down coupled with the fact a gut instinct isn't strong enough evidence held me back. Instead, I said we'd had a domestic incident that got out of hand, I'd run away, wasn't going back and didn't want to be found.

They asked me if I wanted to press charges, explaining that there are now new laws in place to deal with this type of incident. Although I said I didn't want to press charges, the female police officer gently reminded me that Guy could do this again to other women and I could stop it from happening to someone else. I still couldn't do it.

I said I was sorry I hadn't contacted them to let them know I was safe and well and not a missing person. They reassured me this wasn't unusual given the circumstances. They said they just had to check I was physically ok, and they would feed back neutrally that I made the decision to remain uncontactable.

I still don't want to press charges. I just want to be left alone.

I lost one of my contact lenses during that long, awful night, so I've had to revert to wearing my glasses temporarily. Now I'm officially not a missing person, I'm able to re-order my lenses. I'm not sure I'll actually wear them though; I've become used to my glasses that somehow feel like a sort of identity protection. After so long wearing contact lenses daily, the glasses alter my appearance slightly, and with my woolly hat and baggy clothes from charity shops, I don't recognise myself sometimes. And I hope that means other people from before also won't recognise me if I happen to bump into any of them.

Enjoying the freedom and anonymity, I drift around the supermarket, knowing I'm not going to bump into anyone I know. No one judging me or feeling sorry for me. But this feeling is fleeting because overshadowing every minute of every day is the thought that Guy will track me down at some point. That somehow, he will find out where I am and that I'm pregnant and come after me. In bed at night, listening to the creaks and groans of the cottage settling, I imagine him quietly entering, silently treading up the stairs, watching me in bed, his hand gently closing over my mouth, holding it firmly closed as my eyes pop open. I'm cat napping, listening to every sound. It's a private kind of hell.

I start browsing hair dyes. I've always been a blonde from childhood, natural but fading now and streaked with grey. I pick up a shade of brown, a kind of toasted caramel colour. It feels good to be able to use my debit card again. It's like reclaiming a piece of myself which I lost.

I've transferred the money back to Phil that I owed him although he said he didn't want it. It's a surprise and a relief that we have fallen back into the easy relationship we once had as students, but I don't want to abuse his kindness or take it for granted. I'm grateful for his help, extremely grateful, but for his sake as well as mine, I need to remain independent until things are settled between Guy and me. He's offered to stay with me when the baby is due, and although he doesn't know it yet, I have decided to take him up on the offer.

It's a mystery to me why he hasn't been snapped up yet. He's a man who is tailor-made for family life. When I tried to broach the subject with him, he told me he didn't want to compromise and settle for a relationship with someone he liked a lot but wasn't in love with for the sake of having a family.

My brain is swinging madly from one thought to another, unable to settle, as I walk down Market Street: I should probably consider buying a little car, I must contact Kate to sort out the business, maybe I will settle here in Tavistock.

I move off the pavement to allow a woman with a pram and a dog on a lead to get past. The mother smiles her thanks, and I quickly hop back onto the pavement while looking over towards the Pannier Market. I'll just pop in and see what it's like. I know this is a sign that I'm getting better; I haven't felt like doing anything for weeks now. I hardly dare say or even think it but for this small moment I feel happy. It won't last but it's a start.

Standing at the entrance to the indoor market, I listen to the hum of conversation and the clink of cutlery on plates in the café as the smell of coffee envelops me. I feel myself coming alive again. I run my fingers along the spines of the books in the second-hand bookstall and lift a woven handmade tote bag off its hook above the stall, feeling a strong urge to touch the bright bohemian fabric. The thought of settling here is definitely getting stronger.

Outside again, I lift my face to the sun even though it's a cold day. My baby safe inside me. Maybe I'll have a coffee and a cake at Phil's place now.

I look over the road, taking in the lively scene at another café, peering over all the chattering people, and… no… it can't be. My legs come to a complete stop, eyes wide. Short dark hair. Scruffy. It can't be, but it is.

I quickly turn away and carry on, looking behind me to check he isn't following to finish the job. If I can just get lost in this mass of busy shoppers… I cut down the first available side street and stop in a shop doorway, squeezing my hands into fists to stop them shaking. I rest against the window, my buckling legs not strong enough to support me. Breathing deeply, I try to compose myself long enough to get to Phil's café. One foot in front of the other. Breathe. Another step. Breathe.

Opening the door, I see Phil behind the counter with Jenny. He takes one look at my face, says something to her and comes rushing over. Every seat in the café is taken. No one is looking at me but it feels as if everyone is. Am I going to faint? Phil puts his arm around me and ushers me into the back of the café.

"What's happened? Are you alright? Is the baby ok?" His kindly eyes plead with me to tell him everything is ok.

"I've just seen the guy who attacked me," I blurt out.

"What? Here?" He peers into the main part of the café, nonplussed. Recovering himself, he asks, "Where did you see him?"

"A café around the corner."

"It can't be him, Hope." He takes a cloth from his pocket and wipes the clammy sweat from my forehead. "We should go back and see if he's still there. I bet it's just someone who looks like him and you're panicking over nothing. It's not surprising if you see his face everywhere after what you went through." He cups my face and looks me in the eyes, nose brushing mine. "I'll keep you hidden. I won't let anything happen to you. I promise."

"No, I can't." I shake my head hard, tears escaping down my face. "I can't do it."

He wipes the tears from my face with the back of his hand. "We have to know if it's him, Hope. If it is, we need to tell the police and get you away from here. Come on."

Phil pulls his coat on and wraps his scarf around my neck and mouth so only my nose and eyes are visible between the scarf and my hat. Linking my arm through his, we head down the street. We could be any couple enjoying an afternoon in Tavistock. I'm starting to shake again as we approach the Pannier Market and the café. We wander back to the exact place I was when I first caught sight of him.

"He's gone," I mutter, my eyes falling to the now vacant table.

"Let's go to the police."

"No, they'll think I'm making it all up," I say, tugging at his arm, trying to make him follow me back to his café. "They will wonder why I didn't give them the full story to begin with. I might even get sectioned this time." I say the last words only half-jokingly. I've asked myself many times what I would think if someone came to me with my exact story. Honestly, the conclusion I always reach is some sort of mental health issue.

"Stay with me tonight, then. You can't go back to that cottage on your own if it is him and he's tracked you down to here. I still really think we should go to the police though."

"I'm not going to the police yet. I can't, and I won't."

He sighs. "Fine. If you're refusing to budge on the whole police thing, I'm refusing to budge on the fact you have to come back to mine tonight."

Lying on Phil's leather sofa, a throw blanket tucked around me and a mug of hot chocolate warming my hands, I close my eyes and let my mind travel back to the moment I saw him. Was it him? Or was it someone who resembled him? There are lots of small skinny men with receding hairlines around. This one had black glasses with thick frames. My attacker wasn't wearing glasses. But something, some kind of intuition, made me stop when I saw that guy. And I've always told myself to trust my intuition. This feeling is part of being human, and it's there for a reason: to protect us against threats.

I can hear Phil in the kitchen warming up leftovers from the café's menu. Phil's flat is a spacious two-bed above the café, so he doesn't have far to go to work. The spare bedroom has a futon. I'd have been happy to sleep on it but he insisted I have his bed and he would use the futon. By the time he brings the food to me, my eyes are getting heavy. I yawn and sit up.

"It's just the vegetarian spaghetti Bolognese. Plenty of lentils, rich in protein," he says as he passes my plate to me.

When I first met Phil at uni, he was tall and skinny with dark blonde, thick, wavy hair that needed a good cut. He always had a bit of a beard. Mainly because he couldn't be bothered to shave. He lived in typical student clothes of jeans, jumpers and trainers. Like Guy, he played rugby. He wanted to be a teacher and was studying maths. I can't remember him ever cooking at uni. Our closeness strengthened, turning from friends to lovers and then practically living together. I remember how forlorn I felt when we graduated and he said he wanted to teach in London. I didn't want to live in London. I had other ideas then about what I wanted at that stage in my life.

We kept up a long-distance relationship for six months but then it started to wither. Eventually, he met someone else. Later, I heard he had moved to Devon to teach maths at a school there, minus his new girlfriend. I started up our intermittent messaging again, and we occasionally met up for a day in Bath or Bristol. We even once stayed overnight in Bath, where we resumed sleeping together, but then life moved on for both of us.

These days, he looks pretty much the same but minus the thickness to the hair, which is now receding. He's grown a full, dark blonde beard which is flecked with grey, and he's graduated to smart, casual clothes.

When I look back on my life, to the paths I didn't take, not going to London with Phil is one of my two big regrets, right up there beside marrying Guy.

Phil insists on taking me back to the cottage the next day. When we arrive, he tells me to stay in the car while he checks inside the cottage. I don't want to be treated like some helpless maiden who needs protecting. I follow him into the house and around the outbuildings, peering over his shoulder anxiously at every turn. I can't see anything that looks disturbed.

"You can't stay here. I'm not leaving you on your own." He says this in a way that sounds like a statement of fact, which irritates me. I'm a grown woman; I don't need to be told what to do.

"I can't keep staying with you, Phil. I need to be independent and to make some decisions about my future now." I cross my arms.

"Well, you can do that at my place just as well as you can here. Staying here is not sensible and it's not safe."

We stand staring at each other. Although I can't see myself, I know my mouth will have set into a stubborn line. He's right, of course, but that's not the point. The silence stretches between us, Phil continuing his level stare. Who will blink first?

"Ok," I say ungraciously, "I'll pack my bag and come down later on the bus. I'm going to dye my hair, so I warn you, I'll be a brunette when I reappear. I can't keep wearing a hat and skulking around."

"But—"

"Nuhuh." I shake my head. "If you're adamant I'm staying at yours, you can at least give me a bit of space to dye my hair and pack."

Phil huffs. "Fine, but I want you to call me *as soon as* you're done, and I will be straight over to pick you up. No bus."

I tilt my head. "Deal."

He pulls me into a hug, hesitant to leave. I somehow find my cheek lingering against the warmth of his neck, my arms unwilling to let go. As I slowly, reluctantly, release him, he tilts his head down, and our lips brush gently against each other's. I look at him, startled for a second by the intensity of the feelings the touch of his lips has awakened within me.

Chapter Twenty-Eight

Guy: After

Returning home from work, I chuck my bag under the stairs and loosen my tie as I enter the house. Another crap day and it still isn't over yet. I have at least another three hours of reading and drafting for a case before I can relax. Yet again, a long day followed by more work at home, going to bed about 1 a.m. and getting up at 6 a.m. to start all over again. Why did I waste five years training for this crappy life?

I pour myself a large glass of red wine and drink it as I put a ready meal in the microwave. What the fuck does Hope think she's playing at? And come to think of it, where the hell is Steven? I drain the last dregs of my wine. The microwave pings at the same time as a text comes through. Chicken tikka masala, naan and rice coming up.

I unlock my phone as I eat at the kitchen table, opening the WhatsApp message from Steven that's just come through: **I'm on my way to Tavistock. Let me know what you want me to do when I get there. I'm booked into the Travelodge at Okehampton. Speak later. X**

I reply: **Always watching my back, Steven.**

With the TV on low—*Silent Witness* seems appropriate somehow—and a large glass of red wine, I've almost finished drafting the case for the barrister I'm currently partnered with to work on tomorrow. We go to trial in two weeks and he's whinging I haven't given him enough time to prepare. Still, I need to keep him sweet. He's really first-rate, the best this client can afford, and I need to win this case to keep my average up. It's a matter of personal pride as well as prestige for my firm.

My mobile vibrates. Another message from Steven: **Hi, I'm in Okehampton. It's cold and stormy here. You didn't tell me what a bleak place this is. X**

Me: **That's because I don't know what it's like. Never been there. How was your journey?**

Steven: **It was fine. Took about three hours. Just one hold up at Bristol. The Travelodge was easy to find, and there's a big car park and a Burger King, so I'll be ok here. I'll drive down to Tavistock tomorrow and have a look around. X**

I tap the icon to call him. He answers on the first ring, and I jump straight into the conversation. I don't have time for pleasantries right now. I need to finish work and get to bed.

"Use the card we set up in your name to cover your expenses. I just want to know what she's up to. Don't make direct contact. Maybe follow her for a bit. Let her know I know where she is. I want her to feel uneasy. If she thinks she's won this, she's in for a big shock."

Steven must have heard the hard edge to my voice, as he replies as if he's trying to placate me. "Don't worry, I'll put the wind up her. What do you want me to do after that?"

"Let's see what she does next. I want to keep her moving from place to place so she never feels settled anywhere." If you think I'm going to make things easy for you, Hope, think again.

"What if she goes to the police?"

"She won't. I know her. She's scared I'm going to drag her through the courts and bankrupt her in the process.

She's not getting a penny out of me. She's going to realise she made a big mistake in trying to leave me."

"Why not let her go, Guy? We can make a go of it together," he says hopefully.

I roll my eyes, glad Steven can't see me right now. After years of broken hope, I'm sure another little bit of a dream that won't ever amount to anything won't do much damage. "I've told you, Steven, it's not the right time in my career for that. Just support me through this."

"You're not thinking of taking her back, are you, Guy?" A wheedling, slightly pathetic note has entered his voice.

"God no," I half lie, because I'm not actually completely sure what I have planned for her yet or what I want from her. "I just want her to know there are consequences to playing around with me. Got to go now. I've got to finish drafting this case. Enjoy your burger later. I'll phone tomorrow night. Text me if you need to speak during the day. I'll phone when I can. Night."

"Night."

I switch off my phone, glad to be free of his emotional demands.

What is it about the women I choose? I thought Hope would be grateful for a husband like me. Let's face it, her options were declining rapidly when she met me. Pushing forty, living alone with her cat, her chances of having a baby receding by the day. I came along and rescued her. We could have had a good life together. Instead, she rejected me. Publicly humiliated me. It's that, more than anything, I can't stomach. Now, she'll try to get everything she can out of me. Everything I've worked for. I've been through this before with Erica, and I'm not going to let it happen again.

Chapter Twenty-Nine

Hope: After

It sounds as if something is sliding down the roof, a sort of pattering of feet and then a sound like a wedge of melting snow slithering over the roof tiles. Then, a small bump. I jump up, spilling my coffee down my hand and the front of my sweater.

"Shit."

Holding my sweater away from me to keep the hot liquid off my skin, I rush over to the kitchen sink and run my hand under the cold tap to stop the scald. With one hand still holding my sweater, I survey the room for the source of the noise. The back door is bolted, the front door is locked, the windows are locked. No one can get in.

Something small and black whizzes past me, fluttering my hair as it goes. Letting out a scream, I rush over to the table and wedge myself under the stairs in the corner. Huddled down on the floor, the sound of running water competes with my breathing to break the silence.

I survey the room again. Peeking at me above the curtains, from its spot on the curtain rail, is a small bird, its brown feathers fluffed up around its little body. We lock eyes—his are dark and piercing, staring intently at me. My breathing starts to slow. It's only a bird. But how did it get in?

Unfolding myself from under the stairs, I head over to the sink and switch the tap off. I then talk to the bird quietly, making gentle steps towards it, trying not to frighten it. As I lean cautiously over to the window, it flies up and off into the sitting room. Sighing, I follow.

As the bird flies towards the wood burner, I notice the heavy door on it is open.

"So, that's how you got in."

I've only used the wood burner once. I built a fire in the grate when I first arrived here, feeling a great comfort from sitting and watching the flames as the warmth settled over me like a blanket, but I've since become wary of how the smoke could affect my baby. Everything is about my baby now.

I look inside to make sure no other birds are trapped in there. Part of a nest lies inside the grate. I look over at the bird. Now perching on top of the doorframe, it returns the look with a steady gaze.

"I'm sorry you've lost your home. So have I."

Opening the window wide, I leave the little bird alone in the room to find its own way out. I'll finish my coffee, pack my stuff, tidy up and phone Phil to get me. I need to move on and start sorting my life out now.

Packing doesn't take me long at all with the meagre amount I have. Zipping up my bag, I leave it on the bed. I still have a few things downstairs I need to sort through. On my way to take my mug to the sink, I notice the bird has gone from the doorframe. I lean in and glance around the sitting room in case it's just changed its perching position. Nope, the bird has definitely gone.

It takes me a moment to realise the window is now only open a sliver. There's no way in hell a bird could have done that. With my pulse starting to quicken, I rush over to the window, pulling it closed. I can't see anyone outside. Are they inside? I need to get out of here and quick. My breathing turns short and sharp. I know this well—the start of a panic attack.

I run upstairs to collect my bag, one last glance around the bedroom before I go. Then, I'm at the top of the staircase. I stop so suddenly that I nearly topple over and tumble down. An involuntary scream escapes from my throat, echoing down the stairs. A face is peering at me through the little opaque glass window in the front door at the bottom of the stairs, its features blurred by the effect of the glass, making it look like a melted waxwork.

"Who is it?" I try to shout but it comes out more like a croak. I clear my throat and try again. "Who is it?" It still comes out as a croak.

Phil would call out if it were him. Anyone else would knock on the door. This face, filling the whole window, staring back at me, doesn't even move. Why? Could this be a burglar checking to see if I'm home? No, that wouldn't make sense. A burglar wouldn't partially close a window before entering. So, who are they and why are they here? With everything that's happened, I have a feeling this isn't coincidental.

I'm rooted to the spot, holding the banister for support. Next second, I'm teetering on the top step as a rush of adrenalin surges through me. It's a split-second decision. An out of body experience that feels as though someone or something else has taken control of my body. This time, I'm *not* going to be the victim.

Before I know what I'm doing, I run down the stairs, screaming at the top of my lungs to make as much noise as possible.

The face disappears.

I frantically search for something I can use to defend myself; some kind of makeshift weapon. Seeing a walking pole by the door, I grab it. From here, I dart into the kitchen, pull the utensil drawer open and grab the carving knife. A loud thud reverberates through the kitchen from the back door—a possible kick or shoulder barge.

I run back up the stairs, straight into the small bedroom, where there is a chest of drawers I can use to barricade myself in the room while I call for help. A distant memory of an old black and white Errol Flynn film reminds me that I stand more of a chance if I am above my assailant rather than below them or on the same level. The feeling of being trapped, tied up, unable to move spurs me on as I push and pull, managing to get the old oak chest of drawers to the door, blocking the way in. It's not as heavy as I thought. Although I don't know how effective it will be, given the weight, it should give me some time.

Peering out the window, I can't see anyone outside. Then, it's just a flicker, but was there a movement in the outhouse? I stand as still as a sentry at the side of the window so that I can't be seen. There it is again. Maybe it's just the shadow of a bird passing over. Maybe it's not. I take a deep breath. Clutching my phone in my right hand, I call Phil. It goes straight to voicemail.

"Crap."

I'm about to call 999 when I see a speck of light moving along the Brentor road. Whatever it is, it's coming quickly down the road. A Land Rover. Tim? Please let it be him. Searching my phone for his number, I press call. He picks up on the third ring.

"Hi, Anna. Everything—"

"Tim, thank god!" I interrupt. "Someone's trying to break into the cottage. I've barricaded myself in upstairs."

"Bloody hell. I'm in your area. I'll come over right away. Stay where you are. I'm minutes away."

I remain by the window, clutching the knife and walking pole for comfort. The cottage is deathly silent save for the old Napoleon clock steadily ticking the seconds away. A soft winding sound alerts me that it's about to chime the hour. I hold my breath as it, ironically, plays the first chords of "Oranges and Lemons", then strikes through the chimes until 3 p.m. Then, the silence returns.

I glance at the outhouse again. The door is open now. There's definitely someone out there. Please hurry, Tim. I bite my lip to stop it from trembling. I can't see Tim's Land Rover anymore; It must be out of sight on the winding road now.

Upon hearing what I believe to be a car engine, I pull the chest away from the door just enough for me to squeeze through. I hold my breath and tiptoe to the front bedroom. From this window, I can see the Mary Tavy road meandering its way across Dartmoor. Something is making its way up the hill, maybe a car, but its moving fast and I can't see it clearly from here. Could the intruder have been here since before I arrived home and hid his car behind some nearby trees?

Then, silence. Just the clock ticking downstairs and that sound of blood rushing through your ears when your heart is powered by too much adrenalin.

Another engine noise. Louder this time. Tim's Land Rover? I see him stop the vehicle outside the front window of the cottage. I can hear, or imagine I hear, him yanking the handbrake up and cutting the engine, and then he's jumping out of the Land Rover and racing to the front door. I'm already running down the stairs as he shouts, "Anna, it's Tim." He's banging on the front door to get my attention. I nearly fall down the three bottom steps as I rush to let him in, bawling as I fling the front door open. I fall into his arms as the adrenalin leaves me.

"It's ok now, calm down," he says, putting his arm around me awkwardly, holding me up from collapsing.

"Sorry, sorry." I take great gulps of air to try and compose myself.

"That's better. Now, tell me what happened."

Sitting huddled and shivering in Tim's Land Rover despite the heater being on full blast, I watch as Tim walks towards me, done checking for an intruder in the cottage and outbuildings.

He opens the car door and leans in. "There's no one about now, but the lock has been jemmied on the outhouse door. I'll just secure it and lock the cottage up. Have you got all your things?"

"Yes," I reply, touching the bag at my feet with the toe of my boot for reassurance.

"Where do you want to go?" he says, getting back behind the wheel.

"To Phil's, please."

"I'm sorry about all this. We've never had anyone try to break in before. A neighbour down the way said someone tried to steal his oil from the tank recently but it can't be that. They'd need a small tanker for that. Maybe they were searching the property to see how easy it is to break in when you disturbed them."

"Yes, maybe," I agree, not wanting to divulge the other possible truth to this kind, innocent man.

We continue the drive over Dartmoor, slowing only occasionally to allow sheep to pass across the road.

"I'm sorry I interrupted you," I say, staring out the window. "You were probably working, and I've got in the way."

"Don't be silly. I'm only glad I was in the area. Are you sure you're alright?"

"Yes, I'm fine now. It was just a shock."

Chapter Thirty

Steven: After

Taking a drag on my cigarette, I pretend to study my phone. The tired-looking waitress with grey roots in her mousy ponytailed hair puts my coffee carefully on the table in front of me. It's cold sitting outside at this time of year but it's easier to see the comings and goings at the café further down the road. The wool mill shop provided me with a natty tweed cap and matching scarf which work twofold to both keep me warm and help disguise my appearance. The longer I sit here, the more I wish I bought the gloves too to provide a bit more protection against this chilly air. I parked my car at Bedford car park by the river, where it will remain anonymous, just one of many vehicles in the busy town car park.

Something was telling me she'd come back to Tavistock, and here she is jumping down from an old Land Rover. Brown hair now but it's definitely her. Watching her from my somewhat concealed position outside the café, I carefully exhale smoke in small puffs, forming a chain in front of my face. I can't help but enjoy this game Guy's constructed of frightening her and keeping her moving. I'll have to be more careful in the future though; I was nearly caught at the cottage, and I don't need police involvement again.

She puts her bag down on the pavement as the Land Rover drives away. She tries to pull the zip up the front of her black quilted coat. For some curious reason, she seems to be having some difficulty with it. As she struggles, a gust of wind blows down the street. She turns slightly towards me to avoid getting hair in her eyes. I have a better view of her from this angle. A better view of…

"Well, well, well, this is quite unexpected," I whisper, cigarette poised just in front of my mouth. My eyes are fixed on the slight bulge protruding around her stomach, stretching out her sweater. I stop smoking, dropping my cigarette on the ground and grinding it with the heel of my boot, mouth set in a grim line. I have no experience of pregnant women, but I know a month ago, there was no sign of a baby. A sick feeling of apprehension starts to form in the pit of my stomach.

I gulp my coffee back and leave the table quickly to keep her in sight as she walks away down the street. This changes everything. If Guy finds out she's pregnant, he'll do everything possible to get her back and win custody of the child. And where will that leave me? I can't let it happen. Can't let Guy find out. I've waited too long for him. Years of keeping in the background, supporting him, polishing his ego, sharing him with all those women who didn't love him, picking up the pieces when each relationship unravelled. The years of terrible jealousy as Guy foolishly married two of them, but still I continued supporting him, putting him first, loving him. I'm in my forties now—time is moving on while nothing changes. I'm tired of being picked up and discarded whenever it suits Guy. Tired of living in the shadows. Tired of always feeling second best.

No one will care if Guy comes out of the closet now. Maybe ten years ago it would have mattered to his career but time's moved on. We're living in a more accepting world. It's time for Guy to admit his deep feelings for me and start a new life. He's just struggling to let go of the image he's cultivated for himself as a babe magnet. He might still enjoy sex with women but in truth he despises them. His real inclination lies with me. He just needs to admit it to himself and everyone else.

Hope seems to be heading to the café she often visits. Apparently, she has a male friend there. I wonder if Guy knows this. Maybe it isn't even Guy's baby. No, the timing won't work for that theory. There's no way she'd have a bump already if she got pregnant after she left. Her bag must be heavy, as she keeps swapping shoulders.

When she arrives at the café, she turns slightly towards me, using her back to push open the door. I swing round quickly to look in a shop window, preventing her from getting a complete view of my face. I slowly count to three and glance back. She's now inside the café.

I look around for somewhere secluded to loiter where I can still see the café entrance. I step into an alley and lean against one of the walls, watching her through the glass.

Less than five minutes later, she leaves minus the bag, looking a bit lost. She walks right past the alley where I'm hiding. I reach out and skim my fingertips delicately across the back of her coat as she passes. No sound, no sensation for her through the thick material. Slipping out behind her, I notice she seems distracted, flustered, as if she's trying to find her way to somewhere but doesn't know the route. A few streets later, I step sharply into a shop doorway as she arrives at a taxi rank and starts talking to one of the drivers. What is she up to?

After a short conversation I can't lipread due to her back being to me, the driver shrugging more than once in a take it or leave it fashion, she retraces her steps back to the café. I follow at a safe distance, slipping back into the alley to wait for her as she pushes through the door. Within ten minutes, a taxi pulls up outside the café. She emerges from the door with her bag and gets into the back of it. A second later, she's gone.

"Shit." Don't panic, don't lose it here on the street. What will Guy think if she disappears again when I'm supposed to be watching her? I can't ask anyone in the café where she has gone, I... wait...

Hurrying down the street, I head towards the original taxi driver she spoke to. As luck would have it, he's there. I tap him on the shoulder, and he turns to face me.

"Hi, mate, sorry to bother you. I'm looking for my wife. She was trying to arrange a taxi for us, but I can't find her." The taxi driver looks me up and down as if I'm some sort of dimwit.

"Small, brownish hair, black padded coat?" he eventually says.

"Yes, that's her," I say in an ingratiating voice, and I hate myself for it.

"She was here. I can't take you to Exeter St David's; it's too far for me. I only do local routes. I told her to contact Parkers. They do long journeys. She went back towards Market Street."

Eureka! "Thanks, mate."

I hear him chuckling to himself as I turn to go and give him the finger behind my back.

I head towards the river to retrieve my car. If I drive fast, I might just catch them up.

Not for the first time, I wish I finished her off that day when I had the chance.

Chapter Thirty-One

Guy: After

A text pops up on the screen of my phone. I've got a client sitting in front of me in my office. I can see that it's Steven but can't read the message until the client has gone. This client has a drawn-out saga, so I decide to wind up the meeting by reminding him of my fees, which are charged at an extortionate rate every fifteen minutes.

When he's gone, I look at my phone: **She's heading for Exeter station in a taxi. We've got her on the run. Do you want me to get the train or just find out where she is going?**

Fuck!

By the time I'm reading the message, I figure Steven must be at Exeter station. I phone him. It takes him a while to answer.

"Hi, I've just got your message. I have another client waiting, so I'll make it quick." I keep my voice low just in case I can be overheard. "Come home. You have done enough. Let her stew for a bit. I bet she's heading home to face the music. I'll be waiting for her. If she doesn't arrive, then I'll get Rod to find her."

I make a mental note to phone Rod Anderson—the private detective I've used for many cases in the past.

"Too late. I'm on the train. We are going to Cheltenham." He pauses as I let out an expletive. "Does she know anyone there?"

"Christ, I don't—"

"Your client's getting a bit jittery," my secretary interrupts, popping her head into the room.

"One minute," I bark, frowning at her. She disappears quickly, shutting the door behind her.

"I've got to go, mate, speak later."

Steven tries to say something as I cancel the call.

My first thought : how much is this costing me? Then: what the hell is she up to?

Without warning, Jan brings my client in. You'll pay dearly for that, Jan. I can make your working life a misery if I want to.

"So, you're in Cheltenham?" I say on WhatsApp to Steven once the client has left, trying to sound happier than I feel. WhatsApp is a safer way to communicate, as it's encrypted.

"That's right. Have you ever been here before?"

"Yes, once, on a shopping trip with Erica donkey's years ago. What's happening now?" I ask impatiently, steering it away from becoming a social chitchat.

"She's getting a ticket to Tewkesbury as we speak. I'll get one too. The train leaves in ten mins."

"What have you done with the car?"

"I've left it at the long stay car park at Exeter station. I'll collect it later." Great, another expense.

"Has she spoken to anyone?"

"No, but she's texting a lot." He pauses shortly before I hear a loud train whistle down the phone. He doesn't start talking again until the noise goes back to just the hustle and bustle of the station. "You sound pissed off. It's not my fault I couldn't stop her getting on a train," he whines.

"No, no, I'm not fed up with you, it's just work." I mean, it isn't a complete lie—I am fed up with work. But I'm also fed up with him. "Phone when you get to Tewkesbury. You might have some idea where she is going by then."

I cut the connection before he can say anything else. Another client is waiting for me.

What is she up to now? I have a strange feeling deep in the pit of my stomach, and it isn't a pleasant one. Erica lives in Tewkesbury, with her new husband. Maybe I need to arrange a trip there myself.

Chapter Thirty-Two

Hope: After

Tewkesbury is a picturesque, small town dominated by the medieval Abbey, so it's a surprise to me when I get off the train to find myself in a modern low-rise building in the middle of an industrial setting. The station is known as Ashchurch Parkway and it's at least two miles from the centre of Tewkesbury. I booked myself into the Abbey Guesthouse—a B&B in the centre of Tewkesbury—on my phone while I was on the train. It's a pity I didn't check the location of the station. Never mind, I can get a taxi. From its website, the guesthouse looks quaint and upmarket, and it is.

I unpack my assortment of toiletries in the bathroom at the B&B. It's not even worth getting my clothes out of the holdall and hanging them up, as there is nothing that will crease. Sitting on the edge of the large double bed, I suddenly realise how tired I am, both mentally and physically. So, I lift my heavy legs onto the bed, and I lie back. My muscles start to relax as my body sinks into the mattress, and I'm overcome with a deep, deep weariness. I close my eyes for a few minutes to rest, to plan, to think.

I'm finding it hard to make sense of the day. Standing at the top of the stairs in the cottage with that face at the window, I was terrified, but then something shifted inside me, and my terror turned to anger. Anger at being hounded and pursued by someone simply for daring to leave a marriage that was making me miserable. I have a right to live where I want on my own terms, to go about my life without being vilified and molested. If it weren't for the need to protect my baby, I would have reported Guy to the police. I don't care if it destroys his career. Even if it meant dragging him through the courts to account for his bullying, criminal behaviour. He would, of course, deny it all, enlisting one of his solicitor cronies to undermine my character. After all, what evidence do I have against Guy apart from witnesses to his bullying and bad temper?

Opening my eyes, they immediately shift to a moth trapped inside the light fitting, flitting from one side to the other, hastening its own death. Maybe this is what I'm doing? I sit up, switching the main light off from a control by the bed. This will give it a rest and a chance to escape.

I feel desperately tired, depressed, full of regret for all the decisions I've made that have led to this moment. Realistically though, what could I have done differently? With hindsight, there are points along the way where I could have changed direction. If I can just get through the next few days, if my luck holds out, I just might be able to turn the page and start again.

Hauling myself off the bed, I stumble into the bathroom and climb into the large rectangular shower enclosure that has gleaming brass fittings and is lined with dark green and gold ceramic tiles that wouldn't look out of place in a Victorian bathhouse. The hot water cascades over my face and shoulders as I take advantage of the lovely, comforting smell of lavender and clary sage toiletries so thoughtfully provided by the owner of the B&B. The heat slowly starts to thaw me out, allowing my inner strength to steadily re-emerge.

I turn the shower off, step out and wrap the fluffy white bath sheet around me. The first thing I see is my reflection in the mirror. I study the bags under my eyes, the spots that have developed through stress. *Come on, Hope, get a grip on this situation. You can't go on like this. Stand up to Guy. Stop being frightened, stop hiding, face this threat head-on. This isn't just about you now. Come on, Hope,* my mirror image implores me.

"I'm doing everything I can to survive," I whisper back.

I have another life to consider now, and it's my job, my duty, to protect this life and nurture it at all costs. If Guy wants to try and break me, I feel ready to take him on. I'll destroy you, Guy, if I have to. I'll be the one to deliver that knockout blow. I'll break you and your little friend.

I'm sure it *is* Guy behind it all. Who else could it be? Maybe that's why I stayed in the marriage for so long. I hadn't felt strong enough to take him on, to face the backlash I knew would engulf me like a tsunami. But the baby has changed everything. I always knew I wouldn't be allowed to leave without a tremendous battle. My only chance was to plan my escape carefully. To find somewhere to live miles away from him. To make myself financially independent of him. Kate and I talked about it. Of course we did. I needed to release my share of the equity from the partnership. I had plans to set up my own agency elsewhere. How did he find out?

When she saw that I'm pregnant, Jill, the owner of the B&B where I'm staying, offered to make supper for me. She's now setting it down on the table by the window in my room. I'm grateful not to have to go out again tonight. Her macaroni cheese with a crispy bacon topping is just what I need.

Sitting by the window, in the subdued lighting provided by the bedside lamps, I watch the reflected lights from the car headlights bounce off the wet road below. A brief respite. For now, I'm safe. I find myself missing Phil. It feels so normal and natural to be around him. After all those years of searching for a relationship that worked, it had been Phil all along who suited me best. I only hope he feels the same way about me.

Phil was with his accountant when I left my message earlier in the cottage, so he'd switched his phone off. When he switched it back on, he was hit with a barrage of messages. Two from me and several from Tim. By the time I arrived at the café, he was frantic with worry. We had an angry exchange before I departed again, this time in the taxi. Phil wanted me to go straight to the police. For all the reasons I already explained to him, plus the fact we have no evidence it wasn't just what Tim thought it was, I'm not going to the police again. It would be playing straight into Guy's hands. I don't want to be thought of as neurotic and unstable. I can see how easy it would be for Guy to portray me in this way after I ran away, and—this is a big AND—Tim still thinks I'm Anna Brown.

Phil can't understand my need to meet Erica in person. He thinks I should just phone her instead and then go to the police. To be honest, I'm getting tired of hearing this argument and I'm tired of explaining my reasons, going over the same old ground with him. I need to take ownership of my own life and go with my gut instinct rather than the advice of friends—no matter how well-meaning—who have no personal experience of my situation.

I need Erica as an ally if I'm to go to the police, to help me convince them I'm not mentally ill. To convince them Guy's gaslighting me and tried to have me killed. I know Guy, and I know just how malicious he can be in his quests to get his own way. Without witnessing it, it's near impossible to comprehend. And that's exactly why Phil just cannot understand. Not like me, not like Erica.

The last words Phil said to me as I got into the taxi were, "I love you, Hope."

"I love you too, Phil," I whisper now into the empty room, tears prickling my eyes. I only wish I'd realised it twenty years ago.

My mind starts to roam over the past and what might have been. My ruminations lead me to Kate. *Kate, my lovely, lovely friend. My best friend. My surrogate sister. I know you must be wondering why I didn't just come to you, but you see, I feel so wretchedly guilty. What happened was wrong. So wrong. Jamie loves you. He doesn't see me as anything more than your friend and a godmother to his children. I was at my lowest ebb with Guy and needed a shoulder to cry on; Jamie was feeling pushed out as you immersed yourself completely in raising the kids. I stayed round yours to help him look after the children while you were away at your cousin's funeral in Whitby. We had too much to drink. One thing led to another. It felt so nice to be listened to, to be needed and desired even though it was just a thing of the moment, filling a temporary void in our lives. I know. There is no excuse. Please forgive me.*

Do you know what the worst part is? I don't know whose baby I'm carrying. Maybe I deserve to live with this guilt. How am I going to be able to look you in the eye again, watch you coo over my baby while I know there's a chance your husband is the father?

I'm sorry for not heeding your warning about Guy. I should never have married him. I should have listened to you. That's why I'm in this mess now, Kate. It's my responsibility to get out of it. Not yours or Phil's. Please forgive me.

Chapter Thirty-Three

Kate: Before

The alarm should have started bleeping as soon as I opened the door to the back entrance of the building. It's a tricky manoeuvre getting the key out of the lock and reaching the control for the alarm before it bursts into life. This morning, it's silent as I open the door. That's strange—Hope must have forgotten to set the alarm last night. Most days, I manage to avoid this ordeal. I'm usually the last into the office in the morning after I've done the school run. Today is different though, as I had to meet a client at 7:30 so he could sign off the contract for a property we'll be managing for him. He wanted to do it at said property on his way to work. Hope would usually do it for me but she had a doctor's appointment first thing. Jamie is doing the school run, which stresses him out. Multi-tasking isn't a concept that comes easily to him; getting the children dressed and breakfasted in addition to himself disrupts his usually leisurely morning routine.

Throwing my bag on my office chair, I make my way through the main office to the front door to unlock it, then switch the window lights on to highlight the properties to let. Heading back to the kitchen to put the kettle on, I stop to hang my coat up in the office Hope and I share, smoothing my hair in the mirror as I go by. Behind my reflection, I can see the key cabinet. It appears to be open. I turn, expecting it to be a trick of the light in the mirror. It's only slightly open but we never leave it unlocked. It's such a big security risk, and we're all extremely conscious of the need to keep the keys to the properties we manage secure. Any number of bad things could happen if someone who shouldn't gets hold of them. There's a deadlock on the metal cabinet in our office that's now hanging loose. What the hell?

I hear the back door opening.

"Morning," Kylie says, making her way into the main office, shuffling out of her coat to reveal a pretty white blouse which goes well with the regulatory navy blue of her skirt. She's tied her hair up into a loose chignon which makes her look very business-like and older than she actually is.

"Hi, Kylie."

"Would you like a coffee?" she says, going into the kitchen and putting the kettle on.

"I've not long had one thanks." I follow her and peer around the kitchen door. "Was there something wrong with the lock yesterday on the key cabinet?"

"Not that I know of. Why?" she replies, stirring her coffee, the spoon tapping against the sides of the mug.

"The cabinet is open, and the lock is broken."

She whips around, staring at me open-mouthed before quickly following me into the back office, to the key cabinet.

"Gosh." Kylie reaches out to examine the lock. "It looks like it's been jimmied off."

"I don't know. I'll wait for Hope to come in and then we can see if anything is missing. I guess we better not touch anything just in case. I'll phone her and let her know what's happened. She'll be on her way now."

Hope stares at the key cabinet, eyebrow raised. "I locked it last night before I went home. I remember doing it," she says, producing her key. I take out my own, the only other we have, from my compartment bag. We all look at each other, at a complete loss.

"Funny thing, I wonder…" Hope turns to me pensively. "It's strange. Last night, after I locked up, I drove around the front of the building before going home. I had an uneasy feeling while I was here on my own. Nothing I can pinpoint really," she says, biting her bottom lip. "I left the lights on for the display windows as I usually do, but when I drove by, I glanced back in the rear mirror, and they were off. I just thought I was mistaken, and by the time I got home, I'd convinced myself I'd imagined it. Sorry, I should have gone back to check but I was late leaving and you know what Guy is like."

I roll my eyes. "Oh, I know exactly what he's like."

Hope gives me a wry smile. "It looks like someone has switched the electricity off and broken in. It's the only explanation I can think of. Otherwise, the alarm would have gone off and one of us would have been notified. I'll phone the alarm company and ask someone to come out and check it. They might be able to tell us if the electricity was off at any stage."

"Doesn't it have a battery?" Kylie asks.

"You're right, it should have." I look at Hope, who looks back at me helplessly.

Hope shrugs. "You two seem to know more than I do. I've just left it to the alarm company to make sure everything is in order. I'll call the company as soon as the police have been."

The police arrive and go through the motions. They find no fingerprints other than ours. The bell box wires have been cut, so even with the battery, the alarm hadn't sounded. Nothing has been stolen. They note and log the incident but don't mark it as a priority, as nothing's been taken from the office as far as anyone can tell.

Hope's sent emails to the landlords and tenants to let them know what's happened. She's asked the tenants to contact the office if they are concerned about security and we'll arrange lock replacements. If they choose this option, we'll have to cover the costs ourselves.

I've been really worried about Hope for a while now. She looks washed-out most of the time. I know she's miserable with Guy; their relationship has reached as low as it can probably go. I invited her for dinner after work to discuss the situation with Jamie, but she said Guy would make life difficult for her if she came—he doesn't like us or her spending time with us apparently. She's made it clear that any feelings she had for Guy are long gone and her first loyalty is to me. She knows her only option now is to leave him. What did we really know about Guy before she married him? It all happened so quickly and was a real whirlwind romance. Marry in haste and repent at leisure, as the old saying goes. He came along at the right time; she was lonely, heading for forty, wanted a child before it was too late. He seemed to fit the bill: single, no baggage to speak of, good job, good-looking.

It was Jamie who gave me the idea to contact Erica. We were slumped in front of the TV one night after work. Oliver wouldn't settle, so he was sitting on my knee having another bottle while watching a recording of *In the Night Garden*. Every time I thought he'd nodded off, he would open his eyes and look at me accusingly as I tried to carry him to bed.

"Does anyone know what happened to Guy's first wife?" Jamie wondered aloud.

"I don't know much about her really. I think she's a solicitor, and she left him. I think she's called Erica. According to Hope, he was devastated. Maybe that's why he's so possessive of Hope. He's worried that it might happen again."

"Mm, if she's a solicitor, she shouldn't be that hard to track down."

Oliver had nearly finished his bottle. I glanced at Jamie, narrowing my eyes.

"What are you thinking?"

"I've got a bad feeling about Guy. There's a sense of menace about him. Like he's got something to hide. Having a conversation with him is like coming up against a brick wall. It's all on the surface with him. It sounds melodramatic to say this but I've always noticed a threatening tone in his voice if I probe into his background too much. I think we should try to contact Erica and find out what really happened in that marriage."

Chapter Thirty-Four

Hope: Before

Erica lives in a four-bed townhouse in Tewkesbury, overlooking the river Avon. I googled it before I set off to meet her. The invitation to meet at her house surprised me. I'm not sure I would have done the same had I been in her position. I'd rather have met up in a café on more neutral territory. It seems very trusting of her to invite me to her house. After all, I'm nothing to her and she has no obligation to me. If I were her, I'd want to put my marriage to Guy well behind me.

As I ring the doorbell, I study the outside of the house. It's tall and narrow with a gable roof, not unlike the sort of houses I once saw framing the quayside in Copenhagen but without the brightly coloured facade. This one is painted light grey. There's a garage to the left of the front door underneath that side of the house. The area is smart and obviously upmarket. Every townhouse is immaculate in its maintenance. I can't see any signs of cars apart from mine. No signs of any small children or indeed other occupants. I guess the owners are highflying earners who are mainly couples without children. The location has that kind of vibe about it.

"Hello?"

I jump slightly, turning away from my reverie to find myself facing an exceptionally beautiful woman. She's well-groomed, with long, straight blonde hair framing high cheek bones in a perfect oval face. Deep blue eyes, expertly made-up, gaze steadily on me from under her professionally shaped eyebrows. I've seen the occasional photograph of her from when she was younger. Not that Guy's kept a lot of photographs. These are mainly photos of Guy and his work cronies where Erica just happens to be in the background of some of them. In the photos, she looks pretty but fed-up. Five years later, she's poised, relaxed and beautiful. So, that's what leaving Guy does for you.

"Hello, Erica. I'm Hope. Thank you for agreeing to see me."

"Please come in," she says, opening the door wider. The hallway leads into a large open plan kitchen with glass doors looking out onto a small courtyard area. I guess the living area must be upstairs, taking advantage of the view over the Avon and the Malvern Hills.

"Would you like tea or coffee?"

"Coffee, please."

"Sorry, I don't have any sugar," she says, preparing a cafetiere as the kettle boils before putting milk into a jug.

"I'm a sugar-free zone," I reply lamely, failing to get a smile out of her.

"So," she says, putting the cafetiere on the table with a plate of ginger oat biscuits before pouring the coffee, "what is it you think I can help you with?"

I can't help noticing a platinum engagement ring with three large diamonds and a slim diamond eternity ring that I'm guessing doubles as her wedding ring. Her long hair is clearly highlighted and looks as if it's professionally blow-dried every day. Erica seems to have made a successful life for herself since leaving Guy. Prosperity and confidence oozes out of every pore in her body.

I gave her very brief details when I spoke to her on the phone the week before. Enough for her to know Guy and I are unhappily married.

I take a deep breath. "As I said on the phone, my marriage to Guy is falling apart. Our relationship is very volatile. I was wondering if you could help me with something?"

Beginning with my doubts at the start of the relationship, I proceed to tell her everything about the events which have brought me to her door. Once I've finished, I notice the cold blue eyes she regarded me with when she opened the door are now observing me with something approaching sympathy and maybe even compassion.

"Oh, my dear, I wish you'd spoken to me before you married him. We seem to have had a similar experience." She pauses, her fingers toying with the handle of her cup while she debates revealing her next words. Then, a decision seemingly made, she says, "I left him because he hit me during an argument. I was pregnant but hadn't told him about the baby yet. When I left him, I decided to have an abortion. I didn't want any child of mine to have a father like him. He never knew about it." The words are spoken emotionlessly, as if she's giving evidence in court. Erica has locked whatever went on between them in the past deep within her and isn't going to let it resurface now to spoil the equilibrium of her current life.

She takes a sip of her coffee. "He's a bully and a control freak. He was very charming when he was courting me. Everything was so exciting. Once we were married, he seemed to think that he owned me and my life should just revolve around him. He had a terrible temper if he didn't get his own way. I was frightened of him at the end."

Taking a deep breath, she continues, "I've never said this to anyone but as you are here and have been so open and honest with me, I think you ought to know that I think he has a secret life he's too uncomfortable to admit, even to himself."

"What do you mean?" My voice sounds small and miserable as I begin to come to terms with the man I'm married to.

"Well, shortly after we married, a friend of mine saw him in a bar after work with a rather scruffy man. They were having a drink. Nothing wrong with that. What bothered my friend was that the man kept stroking Guy's hand lovingly. I tried to ask Guy about the man but as you well know he can get aggressive if he doesn't want to discuss something. So, I just left it." She starts to play with her rings distractedly, her thoughts returning to that painful time.

"A few months later, I returned home from work to find a man standing at the bottom of our drive. He seemed to be waiting for someone. We lived at the apex of a cul-de-sac, so we didn't have many people hanging about in the street unless they lived there. As I got out of my car, I looked towards him. He was shaking and hugging himself as if cold. He was a skinny, scruffy guy. His clothes appeared to be too big for him, as if they had been bought for someone else. They looked well-worn. I wasn't sure whether to approach him, so I called over from the car to ask if he was looking for someone. He looked at me with such hate that I felt myself recoil. I just quickly went into the house and locked the door.

"When I went upstairs, I looked out of the front bedroom window, and he was still there hanging about, so I phoned Guy to find out what time he was coming home and told him about the man. He told me not to worry and that he was just leaving work. When I returned to the window, the man was on his mobile. He finished the call and walked off.

"Guy returned home over two hours later, which was strange, as his journey only took him forty-five minutes from his office. When I tried to discuss it with him, he lost his temper." Erica pauses and licks her lips. She looks as if she may stop there but then hangs her head and continues.

"Things came to a head when Guy had his wallet stolen at the gym. He was an infrequent gym user when I first met him. When we got married, that changed. Within six months of our marriage, he was going every other night. I could never make firm arrangements for us to meet friends, go to the cinema, theatre or wherever because he was always at the gym. He even cancelled meals with my parents at the last moment, leaving me to eat with them alone. They were hurt by his behaviour and thought he didn't like them.

"One night, he phoned me in a panic from the gym to say his wallet had been stolen. He was in a right state. I told him to cancel all his cards and notify the police. Apparently, his locker had been broken into. He got new cards sorted out. I didn't think anything more of it until I was opening my post one evening and opened his credit card statement by mistake. Thirty thousand pounds spent. We were comfortable but not enough to spend that amount. The card number was his new card. So, of course, I was stunned. We were thirty thousand in debt. All the purchases had been made in the months since his old card was stolen. I tried to talk to him about it when he got home. We had a huge fight, and that was when he hit me, throwing me against the door. He told me his financial affairs were none of my business.

"I left him the next day and went to stay with my parents. I never went back and never spoke to him again. The divorce was conducted through our solicitors. Maybe a year after I walked out, another friend saw him with a man in a nightclub frequented by gay men."

She'd been looking out of the window as if visualising the events again but now turns her attention to me. "I wish he'd just been honest with me. It would have saved us both a lot of heartache. I never wanted to see him again but hoped he was happy in his new relationship if that's what he wanted. So, as you can imagine, I was surprised when I heard he'd got married again. To a woman."

Erica's eyes flit to my stomach, and she rests her hand on my arm. "I wasn't able to have any more children after the abortion. Take care of yourself and the baby. Contact me if you need my help or support. I'm willing to provide a character statement regarding Guy if you need me to."

Despite how painful it was hearing her story, I now know I'm not going mad. Someone else has seen the dark side of Guy. I didn't provoke it or bring it on myself.

I'm ready to put my plan into action: return home, leave him and face the music.

Chapter Thirty-Five

Steven: After

I t's proving difficult to follow Hope from the station in Tewkesbury. I've checked the location of the station on my phone, realising I'll need to get a taxi if I'm going to follow her. There aren't many taxis available at this station.

Guy's so sure she must be going to see Erica. He can't see why she would be going there otherwise. I find somewhere secluded to stand and get my phone out. Guy has texted Erica's address. I call him.

"Are you still in touch with Erica?"

"Of course not. I haven't seen her since the day she left. I did try to contact her a few times but she cut me off. She made it more than clear she didn't want to hear from me again."

"Well, it's getting late now; Hope won't be visiting anybody tonight. I'll find a hotel."

I find a room at a cheap, chain hotel in the centre of Tewkesbury. I order a beer at the bar and sit at a table by the window. Trying hard to keep my eyes open, I rummage through my coat pockets for the prescription I was meant to take to the pharmacy a few days ago. I'll have to find one tomorrow. As the waitress puts fish and chips in front of me, my mobile vibrates in my pocket. It's Guy.

"She's staying at the Abbey Guesthouse."

"Ok," I reply, wondering how he found out so quickly. Then, I remember him mentioning the private detective he used for work.

It isn't busy in the restaurant. Closing my eyes, the sound of glass clinking, the hiss of the coffee machine, the gentle murmurs of conversation from the other customers all contribute to lull me to sleep. If only I could get rid of this headache.

By the time I go to bed, my headache still hasn't subsided despite washing down two ibuprofens with my beer. I hope this isn't the start of another episode.

Chapter Thirty-Six

Guy: After

S teven almost does a double take when he sees me the following morning enjoying a full English breakfast in the restaurant where he stayed last night. For a moment, I think he looks horrified, but then he pulls himself together as I point to the chair opposite me with my knife.

"What are you doing here?" A whiff of BO penetrates through the smell of fried bacon as he walks past me.

"You need to change your shirt, mate."

"Yeah, well, I didn't expect to be on a road trip," he replies, pulling out his seat. "So, as I've already asked, why *are* you here?"

"First things first, what do you want for breakfast?" I push the menu towards him, but he doesn't so much as glance at it.

"I'll have the same as you but order me tea."

I take the opportunity to scrutinise Steven as I order the food at the counter. He really does look rough. And not just because of the crumpled clothes. His face looks white and mottled beneath his patchy stubble. I must get him a razor and a clean shirt. As I continue watching him, he pulls a piece of paper out of the back pocket of his jeans. His hands visibly shake as he tries to focus on it. He hurriedly pushes the crumpled paper back into his pocket as he sees me approaching.

"You ok, mate?"

"Yeah, why?" There's a defensive tone to his voice, and his eyes narrow slightly as he looks up at me.

"Nothing." I shrug. "You just look a bit shaky."

"Just tired. What are you doing here?" he asks again grumpily.

"Thought you would be pleased to see me." I grin but it isn't working its usual magic. There's definitely something wrong with him.

"Ok." I sigh. "Tell me again what happened that day in the car. I don't think you've told me the full story."

"Nothing happened. I was looking for—" He stops as a waitress places his food in front of him, quick enough to suggest the food is already cooked but kept heated. "Thank you." He turns back to me. "I was looking for somewhere to live. You know I can't afford the rents where you are. I thought I would look elsewhere. Corby is a cheaper area. How was I to know she has property in that area? I was just viewing a house. It wasn't me driving that car."

"But the girl who saw her, the police, her car?"

"It wasn't me; I'd left by then. I have no idea where she went after that."

"Forgive me for thinking it's all a bit of a coincidence." I stare him out until he looks down at his food. "Don't get me wrong, I want her to be scared, I want the police to think she's flaky, I want to keep her on edge all the time. She'll be easier to deal with. But I don't want to be involved in this, and it's your job to protect me."

We eat the rest of our breakfast in silence.

"I need a cigarette," Steven says eventually, getting up to leave the restaurant.

I go to the counter to pay the bill. An elderly couple struggle to tap in their pin number ahead of me, holding up proceedings. I feel like paying the bill for them just to move things along. Steven has my best interests at heart. Seeing him like this has made me realise how emotionally vulnerable he is. He brings out protective feelings in me. He always has. He's always doing his best for me, doing anything possible to appease me. Now, it's my turn to provide the support he needs.

After paying the bill, I join him outside. There's a wind blowing over the river. On a warm summer night, it must be lovely to stand here, taking in the view over the river to the Malvern Hills. Not today though. It still isn't fully light at 8:30 a.m. It probably won't get much lighter today. Heavy clouds make the river look grey, the wind rippling the surface as it blows in gusts.

"Let's go and find her," I say as he takes another long drag on his cigarette. "Let's sort this situation out once and for all."

He stubs out his cigarette, looking happier and more relaxed than I've seen him for ages now that I'm here supporting him. I guess he feels that I've finally committed to him; that I've chosen him rather than Hope. As he follows me to the car park, he almost has a spring in his step. It feels good to make someone happy for a change. If I can just sort this mess out, maybe I can find that elusive feeling for myself.

Chapter Thirty-Seven

Hope: After

I'm still getting used to my reflection. Brown hair changes me. I look more grown-up; less vulnerable. Definitely someone you might think twice about crossing. I finish applying my new makeup. A deeply beige foundation helps to give me a more continental appearance. I try a dusky pink lipstick and pout in the mirror. At a glance, you wouldn't necessarily recognise me. I try on my glasses with the new woollen hat. No longer the hunted but maybe now the hunter. If I am being followed, I might be able to give him the slip before I meet Erica later today.

I pull up the waistband on my new maternity trousers. I've bought a large size to disguise my bump. Turning sideways, my profile could be that of a larger lady, not necessarily a pregnant one. Whatever happens, I don't want Guy to know I'm pregnant. Once I've buttoned up my coat, you really can't tell.

It's been two months now since my first meeting with Erica. Since that meeting, I've changed so much. My hair, makeup and clothes belong to a different Hope. A much stronger Hope. My body shape has also changed as the baby grows inside me. I'm putting on weight and not just around my waist. My face is much more rounded, my bust has ballooned and my ankles are swollen.

Late last night, I sent Erica a text. She replied almost immediately, offering to accompany me to a police station today to offer support. I can't believe I didn't know she's a criminal solicitor. Turns out she has contacts in the local police force at Tewkesbury. She said she's prepared to provide me with a personal statement of her own experience with Guy. I feel much more secure with her on my side.

I make myself a coffee, taking it over to the window to watch the street coming to life as the day unfolds, killing time while I wait for Erica to arrive. Under different circumstances, I would have liked to visit the Abbey. I've often seen the car park underwater on the TV during the frequent floods that the town endures during the winter, the Abbey itself appearing like an island as a helicopter hovers over the town, filming it for the national news. From my window, I can see its spire peeping through the rooftops of the surrounding buildings.

How I long to go back to a normal life where I can walk down the street; browse in the shops; go sightseeing; wander around the Abbey, taking in its magnificence. Will I ever have a normal life again after today?

There aren't too many people about at this time of day: an elderly lady in a blue parka coat, leading a little dachshund towards the Abbey grounds; a young guy in shorts and a sweatshirt, jogging down the street; a smartly dressed office worker going into the Italian café, presumably on his way into work.

And then I see him. Guy. Walking across the road, heading in the direction of the Abbey. I watch his long legs, clad in blue jeans, making quick time down the street until he's almost out of view. Then, he disappears into a shop. I can't imagine Guy's visiting the Abbey or that it's a coincidence he's here in Tewkesbury. My hands tremble slightly, causing the hot coffee to dribble over the lip of the mug, burning the skin on my thumb. Now he's here, I know it won't be long before he finds out where I am. I've been repressing my feelings around him for so long that my first reaction to seeing him is one of emotional detachment, or maybe it's just the effects of the shock. Deep inside, I always knew he would track me down one day, that there would be a day of reckoning. I just didn't imagine it would be here and now. The old Hope, that Guy thought he knew so well, would have slowly started to crumble emotionally at this point, but I'm not that person anymore. I'm not alone now; I have something to defend and fight for. The hours of rest and safety are over. It's time to put my disguise to the test.

Leaving the B&B, I hurry across the road. When I get near the spot where I watched him disappear into a shop, I slow and study the shop windows, realising I didn't take notice of which one he walked into. It won't be the vintage interior shop or the women's clothes shop from which the smell of incense lingers on the pavement outside. It might be the pharmacy or the men's outfitters. Catching a glimpse of him at the counter near the window of the men's clothes shop, I force myself to walk briskly past, although every nerve in my body is humming and I want to run away and hide. I can't let myself down again. I have to face up to this. I'd defy anyone to recognise me from a distance. I could be anyone, from a casual window shopper to a busy mother who's just dropped her child off at school. The disguise helps me to feel a little safer, more anonymous and less likely to attract his attention.

Being so near to him again after everything that's happened splits open the kernel of anxiety that has nestled inside me since the day I married him. He seems to have aged more over the past few months, the skin sagging around his jaw, bags under his eyes, more grey streaked through his hair. A slender man of medium build follows

Guy as he leaves the shop. Something about the way he moves unsettles me, but it's only when I have a clear view of him that I recognise him. The man who attacked me. He looks older somehow. Maybe it's my memory of that day. I was in shock. Even so, he looks ill and unkempt.

I pull back into the doorway of a kitchen shop, the assistants inside moving stock around, preparing to open for the day. Guy heads off on his own. His companion crosses the road and disappears up a side street.

My eyes flit between them as I choose who to follow.

Chapter Thirty-Eight

Kate: After

" **M** orning, Kate."

It's 8 a.m. Kylie has been an absolute lifesaver since Hope disappeared. ten-hour days are now the norm for both of us. Jamie has had to step up with the school run, sharing the duties with his mum. We talked about Jamie becoming part of the partnership when Hope was still here. It might happen sooner rather than later now.

"What time am I interviewing for the Saturday job?" I ask.

"She's coming in at eight thirty. I've put her CV on your desk. Your first appointment is at nine thirty."

Phoebe Wells is a friend of Kylie's. She works as a team leader in a call centre for a credit card company during the week. Kylie told me she wants to earn extra money for a deposit on a flat. Saturday is our busiest day, and I need someone to cover the office while Kylie and I are showing prospective tenants around properties, so I'm hoping she'll be a great asset to the business.

There's a knock at the door, still locked due to the fact we're not open yet, and Kylie turns to see who it is.

"That's Phoebe," she says. "Early as always."

Sighing, I pick up the list of questions I prepared last night for the interview. I just wish Hope would come back and sort things out. It feels disloyal to think like this after all she's been through but now I know she's safe, my sympathy is beginning to fade into irritation at the situation I've been left in. I need her. I miss her. What is she doing at this very moment? We've spoken a few times on the phone about Erica, Phil, the baby, the business, but it feels different now, as if there's been a shift in the framework of our relationship. I need to see her, but she seems reluctant to meet up. I suggested meeting halfway. Can I rearrange my week, make space for a trip to Tewkesbury? I could be there and back in a day. Just a couple of hours to sort things out together.

Chapter Thirty-Nine

Steven: After

"Shit." I stamp the cigarette out on the floor before it burns a hole in the carpet. Lighting a cigarette when your hands are trembling is no mean feat. I just about manage to control my hands when a violent muscle spasm in my shoulder contorts my body, whipping my hands away from my mouth. Intermittent twitching, sudden muscle spasms and hot flushes followed by prolonged shivering are making it hard for me to function normally. I've tried the pharmacy near the hotel but they don't stock what I need. They offered to order it in for me but I don't know if I'll still be around by the time it arrives. I'll try the other pharmacy I passed on Church Street yesterday.

I haven't heard the voices yet but it's only a matter of time. Stress and no drugs—a bad combination for me. I didn't expect to be away from home for so long, and Guy turning up unexpectedly has made things worse. Just an extra stress to deal with. If he sees Hope is pregnant, he won't want me anymore. I've risked everything for Guy. The thought of losing him and of a future on the periphery of his life is a miserable, lonely prospect.

I close the window I opened to get rid of the smell of cigarette smoke. I'll have checked out long before they realise I've been smoking. In the bathroom, I switch the cold tap on, the feel of the cold water on my face dragging me out of my lethargy. Sniffing, I dry my face on the thin towel provided. This is turning into a nightmare. I wish I finished her off when I had the chance.

My phone starts ringing, and I take it out of my pocket to see who it is. Considering I know Guy is waiting for me in the car park, he wasn't the person I expected to be calling.

"Hello, everything ok?" I ask.

"She's checked out of the B&B. Sudden change of plans apparently." A cold sensation grips my stomach like a vice.

"Where is she, then?" I say in a voice that sounds thin and high, reedy, feeble. Given that I'm a heavy smoker, I'd have hoped for a deeper timber of voice by now to camouflage when I get stressed. I hate my voice.

"No idea." You check out the area around Erica's house. I'll check the town centre. If you find her, don't do anything, call me."

I end the call. I have to find her before Guy does.

Chapter Forty

Guy: After

It's not hard to notice that Steven's in a bad way and working hard to control it. He's always been secretive and defensive about his illness. It was common knowledge among the group I hung out with at uni that he'd suffered a breakdown before starting. Always a sensitive, highly strung sort of person, I tried to help him over the years. Whenever I got too close to the truth, he disappeared for a while. Seeing him now, walking across the car park, the old feelings of protectiveness surface again. Is it love? I've never dared examine that feeling too much. Have I ever truly been deeply in love before, or has it always been just deep lust? I'm not introspective by nature. I prefer to paper over the cracks and move on. If I keep moving, I feel better.

Steven looks really ill close up. Perspiration on his scalp can be seen through his thinning hair, and he looks as though he's been running a marathon even though it's a cold day. His shabby weatherproof jacket has seen better days. It might have fitted him once, but now it hangs off his shoulders. He looks like a coat hanger with clothes on.

His trembling hands try to light a cigarette.

"Here, let me help you." I hold his lighter for him as he uses both hands to hold the cigarette. Inhaling deeply, he visibly relaxes as the smoke flows through him. "Better?"

He nods. "Guy, why don't we just cut our losses and return home? You can fight her through the courts. You'll win. You know you will. You always do."

"I'm doing this for us, mate. If we go to court, you'll go to prison. My reputation would be in shreds." I put my hands on his shoulders, turning him to face me. "Your reckless actions in Corby have put us both in danger."

"It wasn't me," he stammers unconvincingly.

"I *know* it was you, Steven. *I'm* trying to protect *us*. I could have handled the situation as it was but what you did in Corby is a game changer." I stroke his cheek with my thumb. "I can handle this alone if that's what you want." I feel him fighting with his emotions, knowing he'll end up doing whatever I want.

"No, I'm ok. We should probably get going."

Chapter Forty-One

Hope: After

I circle around the Abbey, heading towards the back of the building and the expanse of carefully tended grass and shrubs in the grounds, which lead to a wall with a gate into the car park. At this time of the morning, there are only a few tourists mingling with the clergy, who are heading for the Abbey entrance. I can hear an organ filtering through the open doors and more muted through the windows and walls as I walk briskly around the outside of the Abbey. I find the sound comforting. The temptation to hide inside is almost overwhelming for a moment. All I have to do is walk through the main door and disappear into one of the chapels. The Abbey has been offering sanctuary for over 900 years. Why shouldn't I take advantage of it? But that won't solve anything. I can't stay here forever, hiding away. I read somewhere once that Edward IV's wife, Elizabeth Woodville, took sanctuary in Westminster Abbey with her children when Richard III took the throne. I wondered then how she'd managed to live there with her family. What would happen if I took refuge here? Refusing to leave the Abbey, using a sleeping bag, food brought in for me every day and then delivering my baby here. Laughing to myself, I imagine the press lined up outside. What a story that would make. I really would be sectioned then. No, the Abbey couldn't offer me sanctuary.

I find a spot to the left of the Abbey where I can see the car park clearly. There aren't many cars parked there yet. The car park attendant, resplendent in his high-vis jacket, is opening up the green wooden cabin beside the entrance to the car park near the High Street. Maybe he's brewing a pot of tea? I'm cold. Very cold. The air is penetrating the bones in my hands, making them stiff and inflexible. Sticking my hands in the pockets of my coat for warmth, I could do with a hot drink too.

It's the car that I recognise first. The new BMW 5 Series Guy bought himself last year. I walk further down the grassy slope to see the car better. Yes, he's inside it, speaking into his phone. When he finishes the call, he continues using the phone, maybe sending text messages or reading his emails? I study his profile from this angle. He's still a good-looking man. When I first met him, I thought I could see a resemblance to the actor Clive Owen, someone I'd had a crush on years ago when he'd first become famous. Maybe that was the initial attraction to Guy. He doesn't look much like Clive Owen anymore. He's put on weight over the last year, his dark hair now smattered with grey and his skin showing the first sign of lines that will settle into a pattern as he ages. The most significant thing to me now is his mouth. I once found it so sexy to watch his lips moving as he spoke to me. He had a sensually shaped mouth, full lips. Recently though, all I've noticed is how cruel it looks. It's funny how your perception of something changes over time, the opposite of the poem in this case: age *will* weary them and the years condemn. How did we get ourselves into this terrible mess?

I pull my coat closer around me. I'm just so, so cold. Guy's unfolding himself out of the car, waving to someone over the top of the roof while pulling his coat on. My nemesis, the skinny guy, is walking down the road towards the car park and passes the attendant, who is now drinking his tea.

So, they do know each other? It wasn't just a coincidence that they were in the shop at the same time? I watch as they stand by the car, talking intently, almost intimately. Guy puts his hands on the skinny guy's shoulders, at one point even cupping his face. It looks an intimate gesture, not an intimidating one such as he'd once used on me, trying to get my attention by forcing my face close to his while he spat out words of fury at something I had done or said.

Is this the guy Erica met briefly outside her house all those years ago? He's still here, centre stage in Guy's life. At this precise moment, I don't feel anything. No jealousy, no hatred or thoughts of revenge. Just a strong desire to be rid of them both. If they'd agree to leave me alone, I would disappear from Guy's life forever. Like a puff of smoke in the wind. That would be the end of it.

The right to be forgotten. That's my dream. Realistically, I know it will never happen. How can you rationalise with someone who can't speak two words to you without losing their temper? How can you negotiate with someone who has tried to kill you?

They seem to have come to some sort of agreement. Guy is getting a blue sports bag, one that I recognise as his gym bag, out of the boot of his car. Slinging it over his shoulder, he heads out of the car park with the skinny guy at his side. In a strange way, it makes me feel sad to see this ordinary item from our old home, a reminder of a brief happy period together.

I head back up the slope, onto the path around the Abbey buildings. I'll catch them up at the entrance to the car park.

Sheltering by the wall close to the entrance to the Abbey, I watch Guy walk towards the B&B I checked out of this morning. Hunched over, the skinny guy walks away from me, down the High Street. A strange sense of calmness floats down like a cloud over me. An elderly woman linking the arm of an elderly man, presumably her husband, gives me a vague smile as they walk by.

Several minutes pass before Guy appears at the door of the B&B. Stopping to button his coat, he casually looks around him. Then, as if he hasn't a care in the world, he strolls across the road towards the Abbey. For a moment, I think he's seen me, but he continues on down the High Street. The area is getting busy now, and it isn't hard to follow him while keeping a generous distance between us. He spends twenty minutes or so just wandering around the centre of the town, occasionally looking up at the facades of the medieval buildings. Sometimes stopping to browse in a shop window. I'm careful not to get too close. Eventually, he stops to take a phone call. Not too long afterwards, smiling to himself, he puts the phone back into his coat pocket. Whatever the conversation was about has amused him. He looks around as if he's looking for someone. Pretending to look at my phone, I watch him crossing the road towards a café out of the corner of my eye. He disappears inside.

What do I do now? Can I risk going inside? The cold air is slowly freezing the end of my nose, and my fingers are stiff and clumsy as I try to get a paper hanky out of the pocket of my coat. It's starting to shred with use but it's all I've got with me.

When he doesn't reappear after fifteen minutes, I decide to risk going inside. I could do with a drink. Standing in a small queue at the counter, a young, bearded guy in front of me is ordering a cappuccino and two lattes. It seems to take an age for the young female assistant to make the drinks. As she confidently operates the machine, I study the menu board above her. So much choice these days. I don't know what half these drinks are.

"Hello, Hope."

Spinning around, I find myself parallel with a dark wool coat. The young guy beside me is cursing. I must have bumped his arm. Adrenalin and fear are pumping through my veins, and I think I can feel a slight trickle of urine escape from my bladder. I mustn't show any fear. I must keep calm.

"Fancy seeing you here. Can I buy you a coffee?" His dark eyes penetrate mine, a smile playing around his mouth. "You must be cold and tired after all the walking you've done this morning."

The beige and black striped seat has coffee stains on the arms from previous occupants. It's strange what you notice at times of great stress. Through the grime and dust on the outside of the glass, I see a family looking at a tourist guide, heads together as they decide where to go. It's an ordinary day with ordinary people going about their business. I force myself to look at Guy sitting across from me at the low table, steam rising from the large mugs of coffee between us.

"What do you want, Guy?" I ask resignedly. So, this is it; the showdown I've spent so long avoiding is finally going to happen in a café in Tewkesbury. I'm relieved it's in a public place—that will give Guy little opportunity to have a meltdown unless he wants to be thrown out. I'm as safe as I can be here.

"I want to know what's going on, Hope." The malevolent look in his eyes belies the casual smile on his lips and tells me everything I need to know about his intentions.

I lean towards him, feeling the warmth from the coffee on my face. "Ok. First, you need to call off your henchman, or I *will* go to the police. Secondly, I want a clean break and a quick divorce. I want my share of the capital invested in the house. That's all. There is nothing to negotiate. You can get on with your life and I can get on with mine."

"That all sounds very fair on paper. But we must remember that *you* were planning to leave *me* not the other way round. Maybe I don't want a divorce. What grounds do you have?" He almost spits the words at me.

"Oh, come on, Guy, we both know you've 'employed' someone to intimidate me."

"What evidence do you have?" he challenges, his expression one of amused superiority.

"I saw you with him this morning."

"Your word against mine." Mocking me. Enjoying himself.

"Or my word *and* Erica's word against yours."

His expression hardens as he leans further towards me, his nose almost touching mine, hands folded in front of him. "You are playing a very dangerous game, Hope. One you're not equipped to play. Let's talk about your new boyfriend, shall we?" He enunciates his words slowly and carefully, each one given just the right degree of emphasis to intimidate and threaten me. Events of the past few months forced me to face up to my fears and move on. I'm not the soft target he once bullied into submission.

"Just an old friend helping me out," I reply without hesitation.

"That's not what I've heard. I think I'll be keeping the house." He smirks. "You're not getting a penny out of me."

"Ok, Guy. Let's play it your way. Shall we talk about your friend, the henchman, or shall we call him *your* boyfriend?" I'm surprised at how calm and in control I sound. I'm almost enjoying myself.

The muscles in his face tighten as he fights to control his urge to shout in my face. I want to hurt him as much as he's hurt me.

"Go on, hit me here in front of everybody. You know you want to."

"You don't know anything about me, you bitch. I wish I'd never met you." A light spray of spittle hits my face.

"Likewise."

We sit staring at each other. A hush has descended at the table to the left of us, occupied by a young couple. Now that we are finally confronting each other, I feel the power shifting between us.

"Let's go outside," Guy eventually says. "We don't want to make an exhibition of ourselves."

He seems calmer. Maybe having reached checkmate, we can continue in a more civilised fashion. Agreeing to his request is my first mistake.

Cold air passes through the door as we step outside. I pull my coat around me, folding my arms around my chest in a protective gesture.

"Are you putting on weight, Hope?"

A shiver runs down my spine. "Comfort eating, Guy. You've been putting me through a lot of stress recently."

Before I have time to react, he places his hand hard against my distended stomach.

"Get off me." I turn to walk away. He grabs my arm, pulling me roughly towards him. Face to face, glaring at me, is a furious Guy.

"You're pregnant. You bitch. When were you going to tell me about this?" The look on his face is one of fury. He raises his hand, hate in his eyes, and then lets it drop to his side. If we were alone, he most likely would have slapped me.

"Leave me alone, or I'll scream," I say, trying to twist my arm from his grasp.

"This changes everything." He points at my stomach. "That's my baby, my child, and you weren't even going to tell me about it."

"No, it's my child." I place my hand protectively on my bump.

"You crazy cow. You're not fit to look after it."

"Let go of me, or I'll make a scene that will get you arrested," I say through clenched teeth.

A second later, I'm pushed closer to Guy, another person sandwiching me between Guy and themselves. I turn to glare at whichever customer from the café has pushed into me, but they begin to talk.

"Don't scream or say anything at all. I have a gun and I'm not afraid to use it," they whisper into my ear. "Just turn around and walk between us as if we are all friends."

Starting to shake, I find it hard to move my legs, which suddenly feel like plasticine. Not again. Please, not again. A wave of nausea brings a rush of bile to my throat, making me gag.

"Shit. Steven, be careful." Guy looks as shocked as I feel. Adding a baby, his baby as far as he's aware, to the equation has obviously made Guy realise I'm no longer expendable.

"Take her arm, Guy, and help her along." Although my normal reasoning and thinking seems to have deserted me, I can tell Guy's henchman is either on drugs or mentally ill. Or both. His voice has a manic edge to it. I decide it isn't a good idea to oppose him when he could pull the trigger at any time.

Linking arms with Guy and the skinny man I now know as Steven, I half-walk, am half-dragged down the street. I hope someone realises something clearly isn't right but no one appears to notice our strange little trio as we make our way down the street. Or if they do, they don't want to get involved.

"Take it easy, Steven. She's pregnant."

"I know."

"Why didn't you tell me?" Guy sounds bewildered and more than a little hurt.

"Why do you think?" The hostility in his voice is a warning that he isn't about to let Guy take control of the situation again.

I can smell the BO wafting off Steven. He's shaking and sweating profusely, his slimy hand grasping mine hard inside my coat pocket.

"Guy, this is ridiculous. What do you think you are going to achieve?" I try to make my voice sound normal but the words come out in a small, broken voice.

"It's nothing to do with Guy now," Steven snarls. "Just shut up until I say you can speak."

"Do as he says, Hope," Guy implores me. I know he isn't concerned for me; it's the baby he's worried about. That and his own future should all this blow up in his face. I would have enjoyed his plight had it not been for my own precarious situation.

A roundabout ahead of us means navigating three roads. Steven's grip on my arm loosens as he focuses on the traffic. I see my chance. Halfway across the first road, the loud exhaust of a boy racer approaches rapidly to my left. Guy pulls at my arm, trying to get back to the kerb, but a surge of adrenalin propels me across the road. A car horn sounds close by, but I don't look back. I keep on running. Running as fast as my middle-aged, out of condition legs are capable.

When my lungs and heart reach their limit, forcing me to slow, I seem to be in a quiet backstreet. A solitary cat slopes down the street ahead of me and stops to listen. Its ears, like a radar dish, alert it to my presence, and it turns to stare at me. We lock eyes, its amber ones blinking back at me. Slowly, deliberately, it turns towards the building, slipping its head around a door, the rest of its body following slowly until it disappears with a flick of a black tail. Looking around me, I see the broken windows of a derelict warehouse, an empty shopfront, the shabby front door of a narrow house. Please, please let this not be a dead end.

I hear someone coming, the sound of their steps echoing down the road.

I move towards the building where the cat disappeared. The door seems to be slightly open. I follow the cat inside, closing the door quietly behind me.

"She came down here." Guy's voice.

Leaning against the closed door, I take a deep breath and listen. Footsteps get louder and quieter again. Then, silence. When I think it's safe to, I use my hands to navigate the wall in the narrow, dark passage I find myself in until I reach a door at the end. Placing my hand gently around the old-fashioned doorknob, I hold my breath and try turning it. I breathe out silently; it isn't locked. Gently, slowly, I open it. Silence. Darkness. A musty smell.

As my eyes adjust to the dark, I see racks filled with soft toys, baby dolls, board games, model cars, planes and train sets. Moving into the room, I close the door behind me. I stand in silence, listening for sounds of any human inhabitancy. A sloth bear smiles silently at me, his big eyes staring vacantly into the room. I tiptoe over to a door in the corner opposite to where I came in. Gently pushing the handle down, it opens, letting a half-light into the room. Another room. This one's much bigger. Empty cardboard boxes are scattered about the floor. I find myself standing behind a counter with a cash till. The till drawer is open and empty. Dust is gently flowing around the room, lit up by the light escaping through the closed, once white but now yellowed roller blinds at the large display window.

I'm in a shop. A deserted shop. I walk carefully over the floor, which is littered with the remnants of old paperwork and abandoned toys. Avoiding stepping on a rubber duck, I reach the shop door. It's locked but I can see the glass has a crack in it. The glass looks thick—maybe enforced glass—

it would take a sledgehammer to break it. Someone has coated the glass with a Windolene substance to stop anyone looking in, leaving a small area to stick a paper notice, which faces the street. I'm trapped here. I was hoping to find another way out rather than having to retrace my steps and risk them seeing me. But at least here I have a place to hide for a while. My options are limited without my mobile, which Steven relieved me of when he pushed the gun into my stomach and slipped his hand into my pocket.

Once I'm sure I haven't been followed, I start to look around, intrigued despite the circumstances I find myself in. Maybe there's a landline that's still connected. Unlikely as this is, as the place really does feel as if the owner's gone for good, it's still worth a look. Behind the counter, to the left, is another door. I didn't notice it when I entered the room.

Opening the door, I find a staircase. It's dark, so I have to feel my way up the stairs using the wall again. The old lino covering the stairs is so sticky with years of grime that the soles of my shoes stick to it as I climb.

At the top of the stairs is another door which opens into a sitting room. Inside is old-fashioned furniture: a green brocade sofa sits against one wall, an old brown rug lies in front of a wall-mounted gas fire, a wooden standard lamp with a tasselled dusky pink shade stands in the corner next to a surprisingly modern TV. Did someone live here? Moving over to the wooden utility sideboard I recognise from my grandparents' house, I study a small black and white wedding photograph, which is propped up against an empty glass vase. The bride is in a 1950s style long white dress and veil. The groom is in a smart suit with a buttonhole corsage. Both are smiling happily at the camera.

The patterned curtains are open, letting in light, which illuminates the dust particles swirling gently around the room. Everything smells musty, as if no one has disturbed this scene for a very long time. I move over to a door which opens into a kitchen. Small and square with minimal plain wooden cupboards. A small, oblong, pale blue Formica table stands in the middle with two wooden chairs. An electric kettle is on the work surface beside a well-used toaster. The fridge door is open, the inside empty. I survey the room for a phone, not really expecting there to be one in the kitchen, as people of a certain generation seem to have the landline in the hall or lounge.

Leaving the kitchen, I make my way into a bedroom. A small double room with a small double bed covered by a green candlewick bedspread. It still has the pillows on it, as if someone tidied up before going out for the day. A 1930s style wooden wardrobe is opposite the bed against one wall, its door partially open, the arms of a white shirt and a maroon jumper peeping out. I search for a landline but I can't even see a phone point. To the left of the bedroom is a small but functional bathroom with a white suite and no shower. A mug with a toothbrush and toothpaste sits on a shelf next to a plain wet shaver. An old piece of soap, cracked with the dry lines of being unused for so long, lies next to the hot tap in the hand basin.

Back in the sitting room, I again look for a phone. I'm beginning to think there isn't one. Then, I see it in the corner, sitting on the floor, partially hidden by green paisley curtains. I pick up the receiver—no dialling tone. It was worth a try. I'm sure now that no one lives here. Maybe the owner has died or gone into a retirement home. Interesting as this is, it still isn't solving my problem. The silent stillness of the room reassures me that I'm alone in the building. Feeling immensely sad, both for myself and the owner of this forgotten world, I close the main door leading to the flat.

As I make my way back down the stairs, there's a noise: a scraping, scuffling sound. I stop halfway, my heart pounding like a piston engine in my ribcage. The noise seems to be coming from the front of the shop. Someone's trying the handle on the front door. I remain still in the dark stairwell. Silence. Eventually, when I hear no more sound, I move towards the door. Opening it gently, I tiptoe into the storeroom, listening for any sign that I'm not alone. Darkness. Silence.

"Hello, Hope."

The shock of his voice feels like a blow to my stomach, forcing me back against the door I just closed, my legs collapsing from under me as I slump to the floor. I was so sure I hadn't been followed and that I was alone here. If I keep my eyes tightly closed, maybe it will all go away.

When I cautiously open my eyes, I can make out Steven standing in the corner, pointing something towards me. The sloth bear smiles sadly behind him from its perch on the shelf. He moves towards me, raising his hand with the object in it. Not a gun as I had first thought—it's too big and the shape isn't right. Maybe a truncheon or baseball bat. Peering through the gloominess shrouding the room, it's difficult to focus on the exact shape. And then he's on me. A searing pain penetrates my skull as a loud crack and a distant scream, my scream, echoes around the room. I fall sideways, my nose pressing against the floor, something warm dripping down my forehead, over my closed eyelids, down my cheeks and neck. A small light appears in the dark similar to a torch beam. It starts flashing on and off slowly, then more rapidly as a long thick rope appears floating like a snake, wrapping itself around and around and around the light until it finally goes out.

Chapter Forty-Two

Guy: After

"What the hell have you done?" The shock of seeing her like this on the floor, so still, the blood... I can't take my eyes off her face, the blood veining across her cheeks, down her neck. For the first time in my life, I don't know what to do. Sickened by the scene before me, I find myself on the verge of a sheer, terrifying panic.

"I'm solving our problem, Guy, because you would never have had the guts to do it." Steven is edgy, shouting, bouncing around from one foot to the other. I try to block him out. Still staring at her face.

"She's pregnant, Steven. If you kill her, you kill my child." The words come out like a howl of pain.

"Leave her. No one knows where she is. No one will find her for weeks. There's a sign on the front of the door saying the owner has died and the shop is closed."

"Shut up, just shut up," I growl—a wolf warning he doesn't pick up on.

I kneel beside Hope, pressing my fingers into different points on her neck, looking for a pulse. I can't feel anything. My fingers, sticky with blood, feel her wrist. Nothing. Blood is still trickling from the wound on her head. "Hope, come on." I shake her gently. No response.

Tears well in my eyes, overflowing down my cheeks. My baby, my child, my future.

An overwhelming rage suddenly engulfs me, propelling me up and swinging me around. I punch Steven as hard as I can, connecting with his nose, the cartilage shattering against my fist. He falls back against a rack, causing boxes of board games to crash to the floor.

"That's my child!" I scream, standing before him, bending down, grasping his hair at the roots, tilting his head to make him look at me. Blood is pouring from his nose and between his lips.

"We could escape," he mumbles, specks of blood spattering my face. "We could live abroad."

Leaving him collapsed on the floor, I straighten, surveying the scene. Hope lying face down on the floor, a pool of blood around her head. Steven slumped in the corner, shaking and mumbling to himself. Anger, hurt, sadness, fear—all these emotions are flashing through my brain, surging through me. Anger at Hope and Steven for messing up my life; hurt that Steven has turned on me when I've always tried to help him and offered years of my love and support; sadness that our relationship never had the chance to flourish, what might have been could I have found a happiness with Steven instead of pursuing all these women; sadness that my chance to be a father had probably gone forever; fear for my own future, which would certainly be in a prison. I'm paralysed with panic. I literally can't move a muscle. My brain, usually so agile, has frozen, like the screen on my laptop. Then, suddenly, the dam bursts… I sob and can't stop.

Flinging open the door to the corridor, I start running. Down the corridor, out the back door, slamming it behind me. I keep running, back to the main street, past startled faces, down the road, back on the pavement, past traffic lights, shops, a garage, a subway, a warehouse, over a bridge, the noise of traffic getting steadily louder, cars flashing by.

My lungs hurt, I gasp for breath, pain throbbing in my chest.

I stop.

The motorway bridge looms before me, a shrouded presence walking slowly towards me over it. This is the end. It's over. My parents' faces hover before me in the air, younger than they are now, a memory from long ago.

The sound of a mobile phone intrudes. It takes me a while to realise it's mine. I pull it from my pocket as if in a trance. It's my secretary. I've moved forward onto the bridge now. The shrouded figure is standing still beside me. Leaning over the side of the bridge, I drop the phone, watching it bounce off the roof of a car, causing it to swerve, then straighten. Someone shouts but it's a distant sound.

I can't go on. I need to defocus from my thoughts, or I'll lose the courage to do what needs to be done, so I use every ounce of my willpower to shut my thoughts off completely like a steel barrier locking down. I'm breathing rapidly as I try to control the fear within me, the cars below flashing by like toy cars on a speed track. One moment, I can feel the barrier beneath my fingers, smooth, cool, then there's the cold metal on my palms, the straining muscles heaving myself up the rail, my trainers slipping as I try to grip, a voice shouting somewhere in the background, my leg over the rail, two legs over the rail, my breathing rapid, rapid, panting.

And then I let go.

Chapter Forty-Three

Steven: After

T he sound of the door slamming brings me round. The last thing I remember is Guy's fist connecting with my nose, a burst of pain and then nothing until the sound of the door. Unsteadily, I haul myself up from the floor to a sitting position and blearily look over towards Hope. She's lying unmoving from where she landed. Blood has pooled around her head like a halo. I can't bring myself to touch her. She must be dead with that amount of blood loss. Good. No more Hope. No more baby. Just me and Guy now.

Try to think straight. The pain from my nose is blurring my thoughts. Wait, if I'm still here and Hope's still here, that means… I have to find Guy. Is he going to the police? He can't go to the police. I've only just got him to myself. I can't lose him now.

Stumbling out of the room, into the corridor, I limp to the back door. Every time I try to walk, a sharp pain like a volt of electricity shoots up my leg. I must have pulled a muscle or cracked a bone in my leg, as it's agony to put any pressure on my right leg. I hobble to the door, trying to block out the pain in my leg and the throbbing in my head from my broken nose. I keep trying to mop the blood with the sleeve of my jacket, but it's no good, and I'm forced to rest against the back door while I try to stem the flow, tilting my head backwards against the door. I can feel the blood flowing down the back of my throat, the bitter taste of iron in my mouth. Eventually, the blood slows to a trickle. The swelling around my eyes and nose is apparent every time I twitch a muscle in my face.

I hear sirens approaching as the cool air shoots more pain through the remains of my broken nose. I let the door close quietly, clicking into place behind me, separating me from the horror in the shop. The fresher air is helping to clear my head. Which way would he have gone? I try to put myself in his position. Where would I go? I stand here wondering what to do as my broken brain struggles to make the connections. An ambulance races past the end of the road. More sirens in the distance help me break free from the brain fog rooting me here.

I follow the sirens and limp to the main street, where people are standing around in huddles.

"What's going on?" I ask the nearest man. He backs off slightly, his face showing a mixture of emotions, the main one being alarm. My face really must be a mess to elicit that sort of reaction.

"An incident on the M5. Traffic's at a stop. Looks as though someone has thrown themselves off the bridge," he says in a soft Gloucestershire burr. Then, "You alright, mate? Do you want some help?" I ignore him, moving away. He shrugs, not wanting to get involved with me.

Suddenly, my heart is racing and my stomach feels like it is gripped by a clamp. Not Guy, please not Guy. I hobble as fast as I can in the direction of the motorway, sweating profusely so that I have to keep wiping my face with the back of my arm. A mixture of blood and snot covers my shirt sleeve. Guy? He wouldn't do anything, surely. He would find a way out of this for both of us. He wouldn't leave me alone.

Handicapped by my leg, I'm making slow progress. There will be a rational explanation, a traffic accident—they happen all the time on motorways. But the irrational, emotional side of my brain tells me it is Guy. The Guy I know is quick-tempered; easily tipped over into a kind of meltdown where you can't reason with him. If he thought he'd killed me, he might have taken off in a maelstrom of emotion.

The traffic is at a complete standstill on the approach roads. Reaching the bridge, shaking, perspiring and gagging for breath, I'm confronted by a police car. Two policemen are talking to a group of stunned faces. As I reach the side of the bridge, three lanes of traffic are also at a complete standstill for as far as my eyes can see. Flashing lights, an articulated lorry blocking all three lanes of the carriageway, a car with steam or maybe smoke coming out of its crumpled bonnet, a woman beside the car crying, three screaming children beside her on the carriageway. And then a crumpled heap of clothes to the right of the car. I can't see a head. An arm at a peculiar angle. A foot in a trainer sticking out from beneath the clothes. A white sole, tan brogue trainer, the white now soiled with something darker. I was with him when he bought them.

Guy.

My Guy.

A policeman looks towards me as an involuntary cry of pain escapes from my throat like the plaintive call of a lonely seagull lost at sea. I want to go straight to him, to hold him in my arms, tell him how much I love him, but I can't go. I can't go. Just by being here now, I'm teetering on the brink of becoming a disaster. Toying with the idea of jumping too.

A woman comes running towards the policeman, shouting that she thinks her husband is having a heart attack in their car. She gestures to a 4X4 in a line of traffic approaching the motorway. I seize my chance to escape. Keeping my head down, I start to shuffle away from the scene.

Numb with shock, I make my way back slowly to the abandoned toy shop. Passing faces stare at me, but I don't acknowledge them. Unprocessed grief sitting on my back like an unexploded bomb. I just keep on walking. One foot in front of the other. I keep going until I reach the toy shop. Stumbling down the corridor I left such a short time ago, all I can think of is that Guy is dead, but my brain just can't process it.

No one must find any trace of him here. I still want to protect him even though he is dead. Dead. If I say it to myself enough times, then it might become real to me. I don't want anyone to link him to this place. I want to keep his memory clean. It's all I can do for him now.

The blood's dried on my face, creating the sensation of a mask every time I make any expressions. The cold air numbed my throbbing face but as I look over every surface, working out what cleaning products I'll need, the pain crashes back through the open cavity that was my nose. Hope's prone body remains on the floor where she fell. I feel such hatred for her that I can hardly bear to look at it. I'll find somewhere to hide her body in the building; there must be a storage cupboard large enough to store her repellent remains. Eventually, I reach the door to the staircase. Standing at the bottom of the stairs, I can see a door at the top. I ponder what could be up there. There must be somewhere to hide her. Could I drag her up there? No, there would be too much blood. The voices go on and on in my head, louder, more persistent. I can't bear the noise. Stamping my feet on the stairs to drown out the noise, I make my way up. The door opens into a cosy little flat. What a revelation. I manically go from room to room. A wardrobe full of clothes. The bed made up. That notice on the shop door states that the owner died. Maybe I can live here for a bit.

I'm not thinking straight. I'm hyper and manic and numb with shock and grief. Falling to my knees, I start to cry, quietly at first and then great howls of pain as I finally let go. I think of Guy. And then my head feels as if it's exploding into a thousand pieces.

Chapter Forty-Four

Kate: After

T he traffic has started to become congested on the M5 as I approach the junction for Cheltenham. It's a relief to know I only have another ten miles or so to drive before I can come off at junction 9. I've been listening to the presenter on BBC Radio 2 prattle on for most of the journey but it's background noise really, my thoughts firmly with Hope. Am I doing the right thing by coming to Tewkesbury to find her? Erica's call came unexpectedly; I hadn't spoken to her since I made contact to arrange that initial meeting for Hope. Relief that Hope is ok is mixed with feelings of shock and disbelief. Erica sounds a frighteningly competent person and Hope is in good hands but I'm Hope's closest friend. We've always supported each other. She needs me now. Will Hope welcome my visit, or will she resent it, seeing it as an intrusion when she's asked for space?

I still don't know the answer as I approach the junction. I notice few cars on the northbound carriageway. The traffic in front of me is now coming to a halt before creeping forward again. A gantry sign ahead is flashing a message.

As I drive on, the traffic still stopping and starting, the northbound carriageway becomes completely empty of cars, and there are flashing lights ahead. It feels eerie to see the carriageway abandoned like this. I can now read the gantry sign: it simply says "Incident".

As I get closer to the incident, I see an ambulance in an area cordoned off by a traffic patrol car. Another car stands abandoned on the carriageway, its windscreen cracked and a large dent in the bonnet. A lorry is trying to manoeuvre back onto the carriageway while the police try to get the traffic moving again on the inside lane.

Indicating to turn off, I make my way slowly up the slip road to the roundabout. I need to turn right if I'm to head into the town centre. The traffic into Tewkesbury is backlogged; it will take a while to get there. Still, who am I to complain when someone might have lost their life? Poor soul. The whole thing leaves me feeling profoundly sad, increasing the already anxious mood I'm in. There are more police cars in the centre of Tewkesbury.

I find somewhere to pull over before putting Erica's postcode into my satnav. I've never been to Tewkesbury, but it looks the kind of place that might be nice for a few nights away with Jamie. Not too far from home if we need to get back for the children but far enough away to feel like a proper break.

"In 400 yards, turn right."

I start the engine again and follow the satnav's instructions. I've never met Erica. She sounded well-spoken but friendly enough once she realised I'm Hope's friend. Still, as I approach her address, I'm feeling increasingly nervous concerning the reception I could receive when I arrive.

Chapter Forty-Five

Hope: After

I clean my face as best I can with a packet of old hand
wipes in my bag that are beginning to lose their
moisture. If I put my collar up and pull my woolly hat low
over my forehead, you might not be able to see the wound.
A splitting headache and slight double vision means I
should go straight to a hospital. But of course, I can't. Too
many questions I can't answer. Walking up the main street,
I pass the same shop windows I browsed in this morning. It
seems like another lifetime already.

Feeling sick, weak and dizzy, I can't think straight. What
should I do now? I have to get away from here. As the
Abbey comes into view, I keep on walking towards it. It
seems to be trying to draw me in, offering a sort of
sanctuary.

Entering the Abbey by the main entrance, I briskly make
my way down a side aisle, looking for a quiet chapel to hide
in. Sitting on a wooden seat at the back of the first one I
come to, I find myself in the Lady chapel. I sit in the
silence, gathering my thoughts, the pounding from the
wound in my head spreading over the whole of my skull. If
I keep blinking, I might be able to control the double vision,
but it doesn't seem to be working right now. My heart rate
eventually calms to something resembling its normal beat,

the muscular spasms and shaking slowly subsiding. A sense of calm comes over me in the solitude and the silence. By the time I get up to leave, I know what I need to do.

Making my way out of the Abbey, I turn right, following the path around to the back of the building where I saw a wooden bench the previous day. The wood feels damp and cold even through the material of my coat. I clean my mobile phone screen with one of the few remaining hand wipes I have left; I can't stomach the thought of that man's hands on the case and didn't have time to clean it when I slipped it out of his pocket as I left the toy shop. Once I'm sure I've removed every last trace of him, I phone Erica. She picks up on the second ring.

"Where are you, Hope? I've been waiting for ages." There's anxiety in her voice.

"Something's happened." I've been in control until now as if in a dream, but telling someone suddenly makes it real, and I can hardly get the words out as my voice starts to break. "It's serious," I manage to say. "I need you to get me."

"Now?"

"Yes."

"Don't worry, I'm coming to get you. Where are you, Hope?" She speaks more gently now, as if to a child in trauma.

"What on earth has happened?" Erica asks as she runs towards me. The note of panic in her voice is far removed from her normal calm demeanour. I try to get up to meet her, but my legs seem to have stopped working and I can't handle the nauseous pain that stabs at me each time I move my head.

"Christ," she says as I pull my hat off. "We have to get you to hospital, Hope, right now."

"I can't go. When I tell you what happened, you'll realise why."

She helps me down the path to her car. The warmth from the heated seat penetrates through my coat and up my spine, reviving me as the car gathers speed.

"I'm taking you back to my place. Darren's away at the moment for work."

Daylight is showing behind the white louvered shutters at the window. I turn my head slowly on the pillow, looking at the pale grey walls and small lights scattered around the ceiling. What time is it? I try to lift my head off the pillow to find my watch. A big mistake. A sledgehammer is pounding through my head, compounded by a wave of nausea. I place my hand over my head, wincing.

The door opens quietly. "Hey, Hope, I hope you don't mind me coming in, but I heard you stirring as I was walking past," Erica says gently as she enters the room.

"Of course not. What time is it?"

"It's nearly eight fifteen." I slept through until morning. "How are you feeling? There's a glass of water and some paracetamol on the bedside table."

"Thanks. I've still got the headache."

"Not surprising. I've got stronger painkillers, but you said last night that you can't take them with the baby."

"No, they advise against it, although I think the blow to my head and blood loss won't have done it any good either."

"We really need to get you to a doctor for the baby's sake and to check you for concussion." Erica leaves the statement hanging in the air.

"I don't want to think about that now."

"Ok," she says slowly, clearly not wanting to push me harder. "I'll get you some breakfast. You need to at least try to eat something. I've left you some pyjamas and a dressing gown on the chair. Then, you can have a bath or a shower and we'll see how you are."

Erica leaves the room, and I slowly push myself out of bed. My first couple of steps are wobbly as I approach the floral fabric chair in the corner of the room, facing the bed. My head is pounding more now that I'm upright, and I lean one palm against the wall to steady myself.

The pyjamas are white cotton with little blue stars on them. I imagined her wearing silk to bed. I'm having to rapidly reappraise my first impressions of Erica. Catching a glimpse of myself in the arch-shaped wall mirror, I inwardly recoil and withdraw from view. Slowly, I bring my face back into view in the mirror. It's much worse than I imagined, with deep bruising around my eyes and cheeks. An image from my childhood flashes into my mind: a neighbour who had gone headfirst through the windscreen of a car. I close my eyes to block the image out.

Holding the banister, I slowly trudge down the stairs and make my way to the kitchen.

As Erica examines my wound again, she says, "I still think you need to see a doctor to get this checked out. You were knocked out for a long time. It's dangerous not to get medical help after a blow to the head."

"You know why I can't do that."

"I hear you but that doesn't mean I agree with you." Biting her lip, she surveys me. "There's someone here to see you."

Startled, I blurt out, "You've called the police?" Please, please don't let her have done that.

"No, I promised you I wouldn't do that. It's Kate; she wanted to be with you."

I can't help myself as I burst into tears. The worried face of my best friend appears peeping around the door.

"She's alright, come on in," Erica says as Kate looks on hesitantly.

Kate moves into the room. Holding her arms open, she gently envelops me in a hug. We stay like this for a long time, me quietly crying into her chest, her murmuring soothing words as she would to her children if they were in distress, in the background Erica boiling the kettle and getting mugs out of the cabinet.

Once the kettle has finished boiling, Erica makes us all a hot drink and sits at the table with a large notepad and pen.

It seems so surreal sitting around Erica's kitchen table with Kate as I go back over the events of the past days. Erica's furiously taking notes as I relay the events of the last few weeks. Kate's face becomes increasingly shocked and despondent.

"Why didn't you ask me for help?" Her voice conveys a mixture of shock, hurt and concern.

"I couldn't let you get dragged down in all this. You have a family. It was my problem to sort."

"You could go to prison, Hope, and what about the baby?" She reaches across the table to take my hand, her eyes showing only love and concern.

"I know." My voice starts to wobble as I try to control the tears. Kate has already been on the verge and now she gives in, quietly sobbing into a tissue.

"Calm down, both of you." Erica puts her pen down and interlocks her fingers on the table. "Now, let's get one thing clear: you are *not* going to prison. You are the victim. It was self-defence."

Erica isn't only a good solicitor, she's also a very practical person. Exhausting myself by going through the series of events again, she makes me go back to bed to rest while she sends Kate out to buy me new clothes. When I awake, I have two pairs of jeans, jumpers and trainers, a pack of pants, two bras and a warm, waterproof jacket.

When I go back downstairs, Erica is waiting for me in the living room with a surprise. She produces a long blonde wig.

"I had breast cancer a few years ago," she explains. "You need to cover your head wound, and a change of hair colour would help. Just do as I say. I have a plan."

Kate sits beside me while Erica outlines this plan to us. At one point, Kate's hand closes over mine, holding it tightly as though she's trying to transfer some strength to me, which she knows I'm going to desperately need over the coming weeks.

Later, Kate goes home to her family and to the business we worked so hard to build together but which will now be her sole responsibility. It's a tearful farewell for both of us. I guess we both know in our hearts that our paths are finally separating after all these years of working together and having this close friendship of love and mutual support.

Erica believes the best place for me to be is with Phil. I don't really have much choice, as she has already spoken to him and arranged everything, but I have to admit that I'm longing to see him again. She's arranged for one of her friends to drive me to Tavistock.

Chapter Forty-Six

Hope: After

S itting on Phil's sofa, watching *Good Morning Britain* seems like the height of indulgence to me. I've never had the chance to live like this before. I was too busy starting the business and then working hard to maintain it. Sunday was my only day off for years.

My head is still sore to touch but the headache is receding and my vision is almost back to normal. The energy-sapping tiredness is still with me though, making it impossible to carry on as I did before. Now I'm back in Tavistock permanently, Phil is adamant that I register with a doctor for the baby's sake. I'm still thinking about it.

The sound of footsteps on the stairs doesn't unduly bother me, as I'm used to Phil coming up and down them from the café during the day, so when he pops his head around the door, I expect him to ask if everything is ok and whether I need anything. Instead, he says something I've been tense about for a long time.

"Hope, there's a policewoman downstairs who has some news for you about Guy. She would like to come up and speak to you." He searches my face sympathetically, and I stare back uncertainly. Somewhere, at the back of my mind, I've been expecting this. Now it's real, I'm not sure I'm strong enough to face it.

"Ok. Invite her up," I reply, removing my legs from the sofa and sitting up.

The policewoman's eyes dart about the room, assessing the situation as she enters. I see her look at my pregnant stomach. She's a young girl, still in her twenties.

"Mrs Chambers?"

"Yes."

"May I sit down?"

I gesture to the chair opposite. "Of course."

She sits down tentatively, holding herself stiffly. She leans towards me, her fingers interlocked on her knees as if in prayer. "I am sorry, but I have some bad news for you. It's about your husband. He's been killed in a road accident. I'm afraid it looks like he has committed suicide."

I don't need to pretend to be shocked; I'm stunned. My mouth drops open and I clasp the cushioning of my chair. We sit in silence while I comprehend what she said. Guy is dead. Did his friend kill him? I can't quite believe he would commit suicide. He always seemed so strong and in control. He would have found a way through it all. It's a strange, perverse feeling but even after everything that happened between us, I still feel as if I've received a deep wound to my heart. A friend once told me that on hearing of the death of her ex-husband, from whom she'd had an acrimonious divorce, she had gone into a kind of mourning. I'd thought it strange at the time, but now I know how she felt. I'm struggling to find the right thing to say.

"Mrs Chambers, do you understand what I've said? Would you like your friend here to support you?" she says gently.

"When did this happen?" My voice comes out in a small, quiet, shocked whisper.

"Two days ago. I'm sorry. I understand from your husband's employers that you are separated. We've been trying to locate you. Your work colleague, Kate, said you're on indefinite sick leave due to your pregnancy. This must be such a shock."

"What happened?"

"I'm afraid he jumped off a bridge over the M5 at Tewkesbury and was hit by a car. He would have died instantly. We have witnesses who said it was a deliberate act. He was alone."

Here I was waiting to be arrested and… now I have to process the death of my husband instead. I don't quite know how I should feel. I thought it would be total relief that he's out of my life but it's not.

"Do his parents know?"

"Yes, we've contacted them. They are at his home now. I think it would best if you contact them."

"I will. I can't believe this."

"A witness reported that she saw him having breakfast with a man early that morning. He was also seen with the same man in a car park not long after. No one seems to know who the man is. Did he know anyone in Tewkesbury? Do you have any idea who this man could be?"

"Not that I know of, but we've been separated a few months. I don't know his movements."

"I have to ask you this, and I'm sorry for having to pry." She pauses. "Is the baby your husband's?"

I nod. "Yes, I think so." I suppose she's gathering evidence for the inquest regarding Guy's state of mind.

She looks at her notes, and her eyes widen for a second, as if she's uncomfortable to approach the next subject. The apologetic look is still on her face. "He was also seen with a dark-haired woman in a café. They appeared to be having an argument. Do you have any idea who she could be? Was he seeing anybody that you know of?"

"I honestly don't know. Our marriage had been over for a while before I left him. He could have been seeing someone else, I suppose." I tense as she treads gently on this dangerous ground.

"You were recorded as a missing person?" She has settled into her routine now and is looking at me as if she expects me to give her a long, rambling explanation, a patient, sympathetic expression on her face. I keep it short, not wanting to contradict myself in any way.

"Yes. I was in a bad place. We weren't getting on. I told the police I wasn't missing."

She pauses for a while, the sympathetic look enticing me to elaborate. When she realises I'm not going to say anything more, she says, "Will you be staying here for now? Just so we know where to contact you if we need to."

"Yes, I'm living here now," I confirm.

"Thank you, I'll leave you to sort out arrangements with your husband's parents. I'm sorry again for your loss. I'll let myself out."

I nod gently, giving a weak smile as she gets up to leave.

A few minutes later, I hear Phil coming up the stairs. He must have seen her leave, or maybe she checked in with him as she departed.

"Are you ok?" He kneels beside me, taking my hands in his. "It's a shock, isn't it?"

"Did she tell you?" I say, still feeling out of it.

"Yes, as she was leaving, she asked me to look in on you."

My cheeks are wet, so I must have been silently crying, maybe I still am, but I can't remember ever being aware of the tears.

Phil rubs my back gently, soothing me. "You don't have to talk about it now if you don't want to. Everything is going to be ok."

"I'm ok. Honest. Strangely, now it's sinking in, I suppose I'm not completely surprised. Everything was so out of control." I shake my head slowly, wiping my cheeks with the back of one hand. "I wonder if he thought I was dead. I know he didn't love me anymore, if he ever did, so I know it wouldn't have been to do with that. It would have been more to do with Guy's career and his future. Facing his parents and his friends." I pause, my hand going to my stomach. "The thought of his child dead."

Phil rises from his knees and sits beside me, putting his arms around me. "You're in shock after everything you have been through. It numbs you for a while."

We sit like this, me resting my head against Phil's chest while he rubs my back and mutters soothing words. After a while, he says, "What a way to go."

Poor Phil. He didn't sign up for any of this. He's a quiet, steady person whose life, so far, has been untouched by any kind of drama or tragedy. How on earth did it all come to this?

"It was probably a spur of the moment thing. He must have panicked," I mutter, staring into the distance.

"Is there anything we need to do now?"

"I'll have to contact his parents. Arrange to get my things from the house after the funeral. He might have changed his will already. I don't know where I stand."

Phil gives me a quizzical look. "Don't worry about that now. Will you go to the funeral? I'll drive you there if you want."

A deep sigh escapes from me. "No, I don't think so, I'll use the baby as an excuse. I better phone his parents today."

"I'll make you a cup of tea first."

I nod. "Thanks. Thanks for everything, Phil."

He opens the door to go downstairs.

"Phil?"

"Yes?"

"I genuinely thought she was here to arrest me. I guess they haven't found the body yet."

He takes a deep breath. "Me too. You need to keep your nerve, Hope. There's nothing to connect you. Guy appears to be the only person to have been seen with him."

My conversation with Guy's parents was a strained affair, as was to be expected. They blame me and think the stress of me leaving him caused him to have a complete breakdown, although there's no evidence of this. They want to arrange the funeral and "look after their son", making it clear I won't be welcome even if I want to attend. From the conversation, it's apparent no one's told them about the baby, so that's a conversation I can delay or avoid completely. His mother said she'll arrange for my clothes to be delivered to me. I'm to contact them via a solicitor in future so his estate can be sorted out. I'm persona non grata as far as they're concerned, but that suits me perfectly.

It only took a few days from there for my clothes to arrive.

I've also since been informed that I'm entitled to half of the proceeds when the house is sold, as I put half the deposit down and paid half the mortgage. I signed the agreement to the sale. I've also been told I can visit the house on a certain day, at a certain time to arrange for the rest of my things to be collected. I can liaise with the solicitor to arrange it but, to be honest, I don't want to go back there ever again. Everything else will go to his parents as his next of kin. He didn't waste any time in changing his will when I left.

The initial shock has gone now. I haven't shed a single tear for him personally. How can I mourn someone who tried to have me killed?

As far as I'm aware, a body still hasn't been found, and the police haven't contacted me again.

Chapter Forty-Seven

Milly: Three Years Later

While my computer screen flickers into life, I amuse myself by skimming through the daily paper. I'm usually the first person in the office each morning in the vain hope that I'll be able to catch up with paperwork before the phones start ringing and my team arrive to monopolise my time.

The cycling event last weekend attracted a great turnout. Over 200 people—double what we had last year. I really loved this event. 200 people cycling from Pitsford Reservoir on the outskirts of Northampton to Rutland Water and back again. A barbecue in the evening. It took a lot of organising, liaising with the police in both counties, sponsorship, T-shirts and volunteers. This was my final year organising the event. When the baby is born, I intend to take a year off. Someone will be recruited to cover my maternity leave, and this person will probably stay on after I've returned to job share the role with me.

Placing my hands around my protruding stomach, I still can't quite believe I'm going to have a baby. Not even thirty yet, I still don't feel like a responsible adult. How will I cope with the responsibility of a child? Sometimes, I still feel like a child myself. Can it really be possible that I'll be holding my own baby in my arms in less than a month?

I glance at the screen still slowly going through the motions of starting up. I have my doubts that anyone replacing me will be so patient with this outdated system. Discussions about a replacement system are ongoing. It won't happen any time soon unless we attract a generous benefactor.

I continue skimming through the newspaper: cabinet shake-up, scandal in the Royal family, a TV reality star admitted to rehab. My eyes stop skimming, focused on one specific headline. I run my finger over the headline as I read it: "Decomposing Body Found in Empty Shop Premises." How sad. I read further into the story. It says the body of a man, believed to be in his early forties, could have been there for as long as three years. The shop was previously a toy shop owned by the same family for over forty years, but when the last of the family died, the building and contents were inherited by a nephew who lives in South Africa. He asked a friend to clear and secure the premises until he could return to England to sort everything. A year later, he died of a heart attack, so nothing was done with the shop. It wasn't until the council started clearing the surrounding properties for demolition to build a new office block that workmen discovered the remains of the man's body.

The old man who owned the shop had been widowed for two years when he died. He and his wife had no children. They lived above the shop after they bought the business from a previous owner. The flat was just as the old man left it when he died. Even his clothes were still in the wardrobe. The police haven't identified the body yet, but they don't think it's connected to the owner. It could be a homeless person or addict who overdosed. The cause of death is unknown at this stage and might never be known due to the level of decomposition of the body. The police are asking the local community to come forward with any information.

The abandoned shop is on the outskirts of Tewkesbury town centre.

I find myself sitting at my desk, just staring at my screen, which has finally reached the stage of asking for my password to log on. My brain, overactive at the best of times, starts rapidly scanning through its index system, trying to make a connection. And then suddenly it clicks into place, the memory igniting a flicker of anxiety.

Tewkesbury. Isn't that where Guy Chambers committed suicide? It was newsworthy only because his wife disappeared for a few weeks before his death. At the time, I read everything I could find online about what happened. It was personal to me. The look on that woman's face when she asked me for help will never leave me. I even went as far as contacting Kate after reading about Guy's death to find out what happened to Hope. Kate told me she herself only knew what had been reported in the news. She said Hope had gone away for a long break to recover from a mental breakdown. I hoped Kate would keep me updated but I was to be disappointed. I never did hear from Kate again. Dan told me people are entitled to their privacy and that it wasn't my business anymore to contact her. So, I reluctantly let it go. Every now and again, I still think about Hope and wonder how she's getting on.

Reading this, I can't help but wonder if there's some sort of a connection. My natural curiosity borders on a strong sense of inquisitiveness or "nosiness", as Dan likes to call it. Right now, I really want to contact Kate Parkinson again. I take a swig of water from the plastic bottle on my desk, healthy living for the baby, while the internal debate rages on within me.

A butterfly takes flight deep within me, fluttering against my internal organs. A strange sensation. The baby is moving. This must be my priority now. I need to drop the digging.

Chapter Forty-Eight

Kate: Three Years Later

It's usual for Jamie or myself to open the office these days, but we're running late after dropping the kids at school, so I've phoned Kylie to ask her to do it. Although Jamie exasperates me sometimes, it's good to be working with him even though he doesn't have the experience Hope has. I miss having her around. She acted as my backstop when things went pear-shaped at work. I can't rely on Jamie in the same way.

I miss Hope as a friend as well, although I understand her reasons for not wanting to come back. It's good to see her settled with Phil; they make a good couple. Jamie and I both like him. We had a few great holidays with them in Devon when Will was still a baby, but I can't see us going to Northumberland often now they've moved. It's just too far. I make a mental note to phone her tonight to see how Phil's new restaurant is doing. Hope seems to be enjoying her role helping out in the restaurant.

The old Hope I knew was always very ambitious and driven. I often wonder if this new life is enough for her and why she hasn't started a new business of her own. I tried to talk to her about it once. She said she and her priorities have changed. We used to be so close, discussing everything openly. Maybe it's the physical distance between us but I feel as if I'm now being kept at arm's length by her. I miss the old Hope.

"Did you complete the paperwork for the Russell Street property yesterday?" I ask Jamie more sharply than I intend as I glare at the driver behind through my rear-view mirror for driving up my ass.

"Nope, I'll do it this morning." He sighs.

"Well, you better hurry. They are coming in at ten."

"Don't nag, Kate," he says wearily. Although we are getting on better now, it still irritates me that he isn't more proactive, but I'm trying to be less of a nag, as he calls it. To me, it doesn't feel as though I'm nagging, just giving him direction to keep the office running smoothly and provide a professional service.

I bite back a retort as I turn right at the traffic lights. "What's so interesting on your phone?"

"I'm just trying to follow something up. There's a news article about a body being found in a derelict shop in Tewkesbury. It's been there a couple of years apparently, and no one knew. Weird that no one reported him missing, don't you think?"

"Yes, very sad," I reply, keeping all emotion out of my voice. I try to stop the trembling in my hands by gripping the steering wheel tighter.

Chapter Forty-Nine

Hope: Three Years Later

I pull at Will's arm, dragging him back from the sea wall. On the other side of the wall, the deep, dark North Sea is thundering against the pier. Each wave seems bigger than the one before, the grey, heavy sky and the sea seeming to merge into one. The wind whips my hair across my eyes and mouth. I didn't want to come here today but Will loves to walk along the pier after nursery school no matter how bad the weather is.

"I'd like to be a sailor when I grow up." Will's slight lisp sticks to the word "sailor". His little face looks up at me excitedly.

"Maybe when the weather is calmer, we can take a boat trip to see if you like it."

"When can we do that? Tomorrow? Please?"

"We won't be able to go until the weekend. No promises though, let's just see what the weather is like."

I turn towards the unmanned lighthouse. A large padlock secures the wooden door which smells faintly of urine. It's a regular destination for dog walkers. Will uses both hands to pull his woolly bobble hat low over his ears as we leave the shelter of the lighthouse and make our way back along the pier, the wind buffeting us as, heads down, we try to shield our faces from the bitter gusts. Nearing the end of the pier, I lift my head to see a man standing by the old lighthouse keeper's cottage. He has a small child sheltering behind his leg. I smile a greeting.

"I don't think we'll risk it," he says, nodding towards the lighthouse. Without stopping, I nod back in acknowledgement.

Will stops further down the road to pick up a piece of seaweed from the dirty, wet sand.

"Put it back, poppet. What do you want that for?"

"I'm collecting it."

I look back towards the pier. The man is still standing there, still staring in my direction. I don't like that he seems unduly interested in us. Even after all this time, I'm still wary of someone tracking me down and opening my box of secrets. The fear never really goes away. Phil still wakes to me screaming and thrashing around during the night sometimes.

I take Will by the hand to hurry him home as he clutches the seaweed in his other hand, trailing it behind him.

The move to Berwick was my idea. Phil was content with spending the rest of his days in Tavistock, running the café. I love the feel of the place and I understand why he feels so at ease there, but I couldn't get over the fact everyone knows our business. Including that Will's not Phil's child.

The idea to settle here first came to me after we had a week's holiday in Northumberland during the summer. We decided to stay at Berwick, as it has a safe beach for Will to play on and it makes a good base for exploring the Northumberland countryside. It's also easy to get the train to Edinburgh for the day—a city I always wanted to visit but somehow never managed to do until that trip.

Visiting Berwick gave me a sense of déjà vu. Everything seemed so familiar and safe. We packed a lot into the week: a day trip to Edinburgh, Paxton House, Kielder Reservoir and Bamburgh Castle. We even managed to fit in a boat trip to the Farne Islands, which Will adored. My favourite time was the evenings, when we would walk along the Elizabethan ramparts looking out towards the sea. I fell in love with everything about Berwick—the quaint streets, the old buildings and the military museum with all its history of the border skirmishes. I took the Lowry Trail alone while Phil played in the park with Will. Lowry had taken his holidays in Berwick every year and painted some of his most memorable pictures there. I could see why he loved it so much. Phil, comparing it to Tavistock, thought it was quite a shabby place really, but I was mesmerised.

Lying in bed one night in the apartment we rented on the Mill Wharf overlooking the estuary, I asked Phil if he would consider living there.

"You're joking, aren't you?"

"No, I'm not. I've been looking at house prices and we could get a larger property for our money here. You could open the sort of restaurant you've always wanted to—specialising in seafood—I think there is scope for a good fish restaurant. There are a few vacant premises that might be suitable."

"That's because no one comes here." He folded his arms defensively across his chest, preparing himself to not like the idea.

I shook my head. "You're wrong, Phil. I think this is an up-and-coming place. It's already busy during the summer. It would be a fresh start for us and a great place to bring Will up. Everyone is so friendly here. And there's a train service to Newcastle and Edinburgh."

"Stop trying to sell it to me, Hope. You're on holiday. It would be different if you were actually living here." Phil turned his back to me and shut his eyes.

On the last day, I wanted to cry as we drove across the bridge connecting Berwick to Tweedmouth, leaving the town and heading back to the A1. I couldn't help but stare back longingly at the Royal Border Bridge in the distance, wondering when we would be back there again. I wanted to live there more than anything else. No one would know my background, no one would judge me. It would be a fresh start. I could finally be myself again.

It took six months for me to persuade Phil to look at properties. I bombarded him with property details, budgets, café and restaurant projects. Six whole months of badgering him. I was beyond ecstatic when he finally gave in. It then took us another six months to sell the business in Tavistock and complete the move.

I've thought about starting up a business of my own. I've thought about it a lot. But the truth is, and I'm only just admitting this to myself, I haven't felt completely well since the day I suffered that head injury. The physical scar has healed. The neurological problems are taking longer to go, if they ever will. I'm slower to grasp details, my speech slurs sometimes, my eyesight in one eye blurs when I'm tired no matter how hard I try to fight it… and I'm always tired. I try every single day to conceal what I'm beginning to think of as my "disablement", but sometimes it's too much for me and I have to withdraw from the world for a while.

Phil is my greatest support. When things are rougher for me, he takes over everything in the home from cooking to ironing to taking care of Will. He's always trying to persuade me to seek medical help but I know they'll discover my scar and questions will be asked that I can't answer. I fear the damage is permanent and will probably get worse over time. The move to Berwick isn't only a form of escape from my past, it's a way for me to feel as if I'm outrunning the deterioration in my brain. I only hope I can manage long enough to see Will grow up.

Phil's restaurant opened within three months of our move to Berwick. A suitable premises at the bottom of Hide Hill that needed a complete renovation. Luckily for us, it already had a commercial kitchen in place from a previous occupant. It had to be updated to Phil's requirements but the basics were already there. We completely upgraded the interior by laying a wooden floor, painting the walls white, purchasing antique pine tables and chairs, crockery, utensils —the list goes on. We decided to operate as a café during the day and a restaurant in the evening to serve homemade fish suppers with a glass of wine for a fixed price. I was afraid Phil would be disappointed that his dream of a fine dining emporium was being sacrificed for the more pragmatic reason of making money. He said we could always open another restaurant later somewhere else if this was a success. We soon had to employ two new members of staff as our reputation grew. I stepped back to spend more time with Will.

As Will grows older and his features are taking on a more permanent form, I look for signs that he's Jamie's child but there are none. He's definitely a mixture of me and Guy, with a faint resemblance to my dad. The way he looks at me sometimes reminds me of Guy when I first met him and he was so charming.

I always walk Will to nursery where we go over the bridge into Tweedmouth. Will loves to stand on that bridge, looking down at the large swan colony floating around the estuary. On the way back, I pick up a national paper to read while having my breakfast in the café with Phil. Today is no different.

"Anything of interest today?" Phil refers to the newspaper as he pours me a filter coffee.

"Mm, nothing much. A few scandals. Poor souls. It must be awful to have your business plastered all over the papers for other people to read. Have we got any avocados to have on toast for breakfast?"

"You can have anything you want if you make it yourself." He laughs, but he's already getting a knife and avocado for me.

And there it is. It's as if time suddenly stops.

"Phil!" I say sharply as he cuts through the skin on the avocado.

"What's the matter?" he replies, not looking up and not particularly interested.

"Phil, come here quickly." There's a rising note of panic in my voice.

He drops the knife, rushing over. "Are you alright?"

"Look at this." I point to a small article tucked away at the bottom of the page, the headline in big letters.

"Body found in derelict shop." The alarm rises in his voice with each word. He removes the paper from my grasp and starts reading it. He pauses to ask, "Do you think it could be him?"

"It's in Tewkesbury and in a derelict shop, who else could it be?" I reply, my voice high-pitched, the words coming out at speed.

I think back to the sloth bear sitting on the shelf, staring into the darkness for all those years. I wonder if they've cleared the toys out now and what happened to him. Part of me wishes I'd taken it home with me.

"What should I do?" The stress is making my throat constrict, causing me to whisper.

"Nothing." Phil shuts the newspaper, chucking it in the recycling. "Forget all about it. There's nothing to connect you to it."

I hate the man whose skeleton they found but even I have to admit it's upsetting someone could go missing for so many years and no one notice.

"I'm going for a long walk. I need to clear my head."

"Don't dwell on it, Hope. It won't do you any good." Phil is back to his pragmatic self.

"I'll be back soon," I call over my shoulder as I head out the door of our café.

I find a seat on the Elizabethan walls not far from the Main Guard, where I can see the lighthouse protruding out of the sea. The wind is picking up. A couple of seagulls call overhead as they circle around, looking for food. Pulling my collar up around my ears, my thoughts take me back to the day it all started.

"Just talk me through the events as they happened, Hope." We were sitting at Erica's kitchen table. She had a notepad in front of her, which I didn't register as strange at the time but I wasn't thinking straight back then.

"Kylie made the appointment for me. I checked the appointment book when I arrived for work. I had two people viewing the same property exactly one hour apart. I'd have to kill time between; it wouldn't be worth coming back to the office. One was a young girl in her twenties that I'd shown another property to the week before. The other was a man called Mr Foster. I didn't know him. I had to look up his details before the appointment."

Chapter Fifty

Hope: Before

"Kylie, did you meet Mr Foster when he made the appointment?"

She looks up from her screen, frowning, trying to remember. "No," she says eventually. "He made the appointment over the phone."

"Do we know anything about him?"

"Not really. He's just looking for a property in Corby for under five hundred and fifty a month. That's the maximum he can afford. He's staying with friends at the moment. The mobile number is there if you want to give him a ring."

"Ok, thanks."

I decide not to call him and instead go straight to the property. I arrive there early to have a good look around. Kate did the initial viewing with the landlord, so I haven't had the opportunity to view it for myself. From what I've been told, it's a nice little two-bed terraced house in a quiet location. It desperately needs redecorating, the carpets need replacing and the bathroom suite is dated. That's why it's being marketed for a lower rental.

Caroline, the first viewing, is a lovely girl who needs to live in Corby within walking distance of the town centre. She's started her first job at the Arts Centre, doesn't have access to transport and wants to be near the centre for socialising. Her budget is very small. She would be struggling to pay the rent, even with this property. She arrives early for her viewing.

"I really like it. It's a perfect location," she says as I show her around. "The rent will be a bit of a struggle though."

"You have to factor in the bills as well and Council tax," I remind her.

"Do you think the landlord would negotiate the rent?"

I smile at her innocence. "No, he won't. I'm afraid it doesn't work like that," I say gently. "It's already reduced because of the condition. I can advise the landlord on what I think is reasonable but the final decision rests with him."

She twists her mouth to the side in thought. "Ok. I'll take it. I'll just about be able to manage."

"That's great. I'll let the office know. The paperwork will be emailed to you later today. Can you let me have it back asap so that we can start the credit and reference checks?"

We part company, she going back to work, I remaining at the property to phone the office and most importantly to phone Mr Foster to let him know that the property is now, dependant on the credit and reference checks, let.

"Have we got anything else we can offer Mr Foster?"

"Not at that price I don't think." I hear Kylie tapping on her keyboard, looking for other properties. "Nope. Sorry. There's nothing we can offer."

"Ok. I'll phone him and cancel the appointment, then I'll head back to the office."

"See you later."

Mr Foster's mobile number goes straight to voicemail, so I leave a message.

Chapter Fifty-One

Hope: After

"Do you want a break now?" Erica pauses her note-taking, her expensive-looking ballpoint pen hovering over her neat, strong handwriting. She looks concerned, and I realise I've been crying again in the weird silent way that seems to come over me unexpectedly since this all started.

"Shall I make a cup of tea?" she says when I continue to silently stare into space. When I fail to answer, she gets up and makes it anyway. Words continue to fail me as I fixate on a small scuff on the wall, my eyes stuck there for minutes.

"I know that this must be very hard for you. Just take your time," Erica says as she puts a strong cup of tea in front of me. "If it helps to think and talk about it in the abstract, then let's tackle it that way. Just continue when you are ready."

I take a deep breath. "The street was quiet as I left the property. I didn't see anyone. I remember thinking that this was a good opportunity to pop into a supermarket so that I didn't have to stop on the way home that night. I didn't want Guy complaining again about me being late."

Erica nods, clearly understanding how his moods could swing.

"I felt in a good mood as I came out of the Tesco Extra about two miles away from the office. I remember thinking that I could spare an hour out of the office for myself. Time on my own was rare those days. Just an hour to myself would lift my spirits. I opened the boot of my car to put the shopping in, and that's when it happened." I gulped.

"A man came up very close to me and said, 'Don't move, I have a gun. Just do as I say. I'll be right behind you.' I didn't even have time to scream. He maneuvered me into the passenger seat of a car, which was parked next to mine. Slamming the door, locking me in. When he opened the driver's door"—I stop, breathe in, breathe out, breathe in, breathe out, trying to keep a calm composure—"the gun was pointing at me.

"He kept the gun on his knee as he drove. I had no idea if it was real or a toy gun, but it looked real. I asked him what he wanted with me. I decided that maybe that was it—how it would end. He told me to shut up, not once taking his eyes off the road.

"I remember he was driving very fast. He was a skinny man, with a baseball cap pulled low over his forehead. He vaguely smelled of BO. I tried to keep my wits about me to remember details. I was shaking and crying a lot, this constant coldness in me.

"We pulled up at a roundabout very suddenly. It threw me forward in my seat, causing the seatbelt to cut into my neck." I place my hand on my neck where the cut had been, remembering the sharp burning pain on my skin as it had been inflicted. "I think he intended to go straight over without stopping but another car—a Micra, I think—was crossing very slowly ahead of us, forcing him to stop.

"I remember thinking that could be an opportunity to jump out, but when I tried the handle, it was locked. He noticed, pointed the gun at my stomach and told me not to try anything. I remember this next bit very clearly. I turned my head to see the car next to me. A young woman was looking directly at me. Short dark hair. A pixie cut." I smile at the memory. "Her face is ingrained in my brain. Without really thinking and running out of options, I silently mouthed, 'Please help me.' He rammed the accelerator and we shot off over the roundabout.

"I kept looking in the wing mirror. The woman was following. It was a great comfort to me. A glimmer of hope. It wasn't until we got near to the house that it dawned on me where we were going. I hadn't been able to see the woman's car for a while. And that's the point when I thought maybe she hadn't been following us after all.

"He parked near to the house. I remember it was street parking and that was the nearest space. The street was deserted. As he opened the car door, I could see the gun pointing at me, almost completely concealed by his jacket. It was then that I noticed the woman's car coming slowly down the street, and my glimmer of hope was back. But he also noticed she was following. He tightened his grip on my arm and told me to get in the house quickly.

"That woman saved my life." I grin through silent tears. "He started panicking. He was sweating profusely. His hands were damp with sweat. I remember thinking that he might have high blood pressure. I think I'd read somewhere that damp, clammy hands could be a symptom. Funny what goes through your mind when you think you're about to die." I laugh but there's no humour to it.

"He hustled me down the path. I remember tripping up. He had his own keys to the house. It wasn't until much later that I remembered the break in at the office." I frown. "He must have been the one who did it. He must have copied the keys. I don't know. I wasn't thinking straight at that moment. All sorts of fears were rushing through my mind.

"When we got into the house, he took me into the kitchen. There was a padlocked door to a cellar where the owner stored some of his own stuff. I'd never been down there. It was concealed behind a large free-standing Welsh dresser that I'd presumed was installed because the kitchen was very basic and didn't have enough cupboard space. He had a key, opened the door and shoved me down the stairs. They were slightly damp... slippery. I remember brushing the walls with my fingers to stop myself falling, feeling the damp, slimy material.

"He had already prepared everything down there: rope, masking tape, plastic tapes. He tied me up, hands and feet, and taped my mouth." I swallow hard then take a deep breath. "He made me lie on the floor, which smelt and felt very damp." I pause and shake my head.

Erica reaches over with her free hand and squeezes mine. "It's ok. You're ok now."

"I thought he was going to rape me.

"I saw him go back upstairs with the padlock. There was shuffling as I assume he moved the dresser back in place. Then, I could hear him locking the padlock, I guess from the inside, although I'd noticed a mortice lock on the door. I heard a bolt go across, into place. Then, he came back down."

I looked at the table, ashamed, unable to make eye contact with Erica. "I was involuntarily wetting myself as he approached me. I remember the warm wet dribbling down my legs and the smell of my own urine. He slapped my face, hard." I touched my cheek. "Right here. I started crying again. He called me a bitch and told me to shut up. I could see in his eyes how much he despised me, and I had no clue why.

"Then, he pulled a plastic bag out of his pocket. He tried to cover my face, my mouth and nose with it." I have to take deep breaths, as if I'm back in that moment, unable to breathe again. "I tried to move my head, but I couldn't get away from it. That's when I heard the front door crash open and a voice calling, 'Police.' I remember him quickly moving over towards the back of the room behind the landlord's pile of junk and then he just... disappeared.

"I could hear the police above moving about and calling, the sound of their radios, but I couldn't move or speak.

"After what seemed like a very short time, it all went quiet, and I was left alone in the cellar. I waited a long time for someone to come back and rescue me, but they never did.

"I wasn't sure where he was—if he was still in the cellar or hiding just outside. I'd never been in the back garden, just seen it from the window. I tried to think of the layout and what I could do to defend myself if he came back. I lay there alone in the dark and the silence, listening, waiting on the cold, hard floor. I tried not to think about the cramps in my arms and legs. I simply tried to calm myself. To prepare myself for what was potentially to come. I knew I had to try and escape." I pause momentarily as Erica turns the page in her notepad for the third time. I take myself out of my memory to wonder how she manages to jot notes so quickly.

"In his rush to secure me, he hadn't tied my feet properly. I managed to release my legs by rubbing my ankles against the plastic until it sprang open. I was able to stand up. I started to explore the cellar, my hands still tied behind my back, my mouth still taped closed. The landlord's junk pile had some gardening tools. I manoeuvred a pair of shears with my feet out of the pile, dislodging everything else. The noise seemed deafening to me. I was sure someone would hear it and come. I didn't know if he was still nearby. I stood in silence, listening, but nothing happened.

"During the next... I don't know how long, the hours seemed to be the longest of my life, I moved the rope tied around my wrists back and forth over the open shears. Eventually, I managed to free myself." I catch Erica peering at my wrists, maybe looking for scars or any remnant of the event. "I still thought he might come back.

"I was searching in the dark, crawling on my hands and knees. I made my way to the area where I thought he had disappeared. There was an old coal chute leading back to the surface. It had been padlocked from the outside at one time, but it wasn't now. I clawed my way up the chute using my hands and feet for leverage. I fell back into the cellar a few times, cutting my fingers as I scrabbled for a hold on the brickwork. Eventually, I managed to get to the top. There was something heavy keeping the lid down. It took all my strength to push it off. It looked like a concrete slab used on patios. Then, I noticed that a path had been laid over the top of the entrance. The slab had been part of that.

"I was crying and shouting for help, but no one came. The chute lid was on a hinge. As I climbed up through the hole, it sprang back down, gashing my leg." An image of the scar on my leg flashes into my mind. "It was starting to get light again by that time. I found myself in the back garden. I didn't have my mobile. I have no idea what happened to it. My purse was still in my coat pocket.

"I wasn't thinking straight but I knew I had to get away. There was a fence—it was broken in places, the rotting panel foundations loose. I remember thinking that after everything that had gone on between us, Guy must have hired someone to kill me and that I must get away from the area. Get as far away from him as I could. If he was capable of organising this, he would come after me again if he knew I was still alive.

"I walked to the station. The concourse was quiet at that time of the day, with only a few people around. I used the disabled toilet to clean myself up. I quickly splashed water on my face then filled the sink with soapy water to rinse the crotch of my trousers and pants, trying to get the urine smell out, before drying them as best I could with the hand dryer. You can't imagine what a state I was in or how grateful I was to be standing in that toilet. I was alive. I'd escaped. I suppose I was in a state of deep shock, just focusing on survival.

"I bought a ticket and got on the train. As it pulled out of the station, all I wanted was to hide, to disappear forever to a place where no one would ever find me again."

Chapter Fifty-Two

Erica: Three Years Later

The reception area is heaving with court staff, prosecutors, solicitors, defendants, family and friends. I'm so used to it now; I hardly notice the noise. Pulling my phone from my bag as I head for the exit, I check for any messages from the office. There's one from Pam: Can you phone the barrister regarding the forthcoming case you have in the Crown Court next Tuesday?

I smile weakly to myself, thinking back to the aspiration I once had to be a barrister. Guy put a stop to that dream. My life changed completely from the day I left him. Just like so much else in my life since. It took a while for me to process what had happened in our marriage. Gradually, over time, as I came to terms with it, I realised that I wasn't the same woman I was at the beginning of the relationship. Through a mixture of birth, genes and education, I'm lucky I could take care of myself both financially and emotionally, but there are others out there in the same situation as me who don't have those options.

As I'm about to leave the building by a side door, I notice a copy of the local paper discarded on a bench, the words "body" and "shop" catching my attention. I continue walking and tilt my head up at the grey heavy cloud, a fine drizzle kissing my face as I step out into the damp, gloomy afternoon. My car is parked in the secure car park at the back of the court building. The words "body" and "shop" remain at the forefront of my mind as I pace the pavement, my briefcase over my head. Why won't those damn words leave my brain?

"For crying out loud," I moan to myself as I turn around and head back into the building. The paper's still there. I pick it up, sitting on the bench to scan the page. The shoulders of my coat are already damp from the drizzle, my hair sprinkled with rain like a mist, the briefcase having done a useless job against the breeze blowing the light rain. Unfolding the paper, I see a photo of a shabby shopfront. I can just make out the notice still attached to the inside of the door.

After Hope went back to Tavistock, I visited the street where it happened. Making myself walk past the shopfront to look for signs of activity, I can still remember the eerie feeling as I looked up towards the window of the flat above, knowing that in that room lay the body of a man I'd once met fleetingly. So many questions were running through my mind at the time. Had I made the right decision? What about all my professional training, my internal moral compass and strict law-abiding upbringing? Did those count for nothing? Could I live with that knowledge for the rest of my life? What would happen when the body was found? Would there be any connection to Hope?

The police made a visit to me at work a few days after Guy died. They'd made the connection between us, seen the coincidence that he'd been in Tewkesbury. I was able to truthfully say I hadn't seen or heard from him in years and had no idea why he was there or why he killed himself. I had an alibi. I'd been in the office when he died. I didn't hear from the police again.

After all this time, they might still be able to make the connection between Steven and Guy. Probably not but even if they do it will only add to the mystery of Guy's suicide. But no, that can't happen; I've covered all the bases. Hope will be ok. I've done the right thing.

I look up from the newspaper at the sound of shouting. Two youths, due to appear in court, squaring up to each other. The court security staff are soon dealing with it. Why do people have to make such a mess of their lives? Since joining the practice in Tewkesbury, I've chosen to specialise in domestic abuse cases. The hidden misery going on behind closed doors. I've seen it all: emotional abuse, physical abuse. All types of people from all walks of life. I've even experienced some of it myself at the hands of Guy.

I look back at the paper in my hands. Did I do the right thing? Hope would never have survived imprisonment, the bail conditions, the long hours in court being savaged on all aspects of her life. Any barrister would have torn her to shreds. No matter how sympathetic the jury may have been, she would have faced a prison sentence, and for what? For marrying the wrong man, for trying to leave him, for standing up for herself and her baby. Hope's baby. Was that the thing that made the decision for me? It could have been me.

Pressing my lips together, I swallow the threat of tears. After all these years, I still feel the deep pain of saying goodbye to my chance of motherhood.

Mitch Sweeney was one of my clients. To look at him, you would think he doesn't have a care in the world. The day he walked into my office and sat in the chair opposite, I thought maybe Pam had given me the file for the wrong client. A tall, dark-haired, attractive guy. He was smiley and seemed relaxed. As I listened to him describe the level of emotional and physical abuse he was suffering at home, I re-evaluated my first impression. Here was a man who regularly had hot food poured over him if he dared to say a word out of place. He had cigarette burns on his back and shoulders. A large bruise on his ribs as the result of being hit with a garden rake. When he was at work, his wife phoned him between ten and twenty times a day to find out where he was. All his friends had been frozen out of his life. And yet he remained loyal to her, blaming the problems on her mental health.

"I don't know what would happen to her if I wasn't around to take care of her."

It was difficult to comprehend how he could continue to defend her. But I'd seen this reaction before. It was almost as if he'd been groomed to accept it as his own fault; that he'd made her do these things to him.

"So, why are you here, Mr Sweeney?"

He put his head in his hands and started to quietly cry. "I just can't take it anymore," he finally managed to say.

The decision to leave his home and everything he'd worked for was crushing for him despite the level of abuse. He really thought it might be his fault she behaved like that. He was ashamed that he couldn't deal with the situation himself and didn't want to ask his friends for help.

I made the call myself to one of his old friends, who agreed to let him stay at his home until the situation was sorted. Even after the divorce, he still paid her mortgage and her bills until he realised another man had moved in. It was only then he felt he could finally move on.

I've always been careful not to let myself get emotionally involved in my clients' affairs, but this case stayed with me long after the proceedings were over. As Mitch works for a local building firm, I still see him now and again in passing. I know he's now living with a woman who works at a veterinary practice. When I asked him if he'd do me a favour, he replied, "Anything, just name it." He understood straight away when I explained the situation and what I needed him to do. We haven't spoken about it since.

Gently laying the newspaper back on the bench where I found it, I pull my coat tightly around me as I head for the side exit.

I *did* do the right thing.

'*A body was found in Mason's Toy Shop in Chance Street, which had been closed for a number of years following the death of the owner. The body was discovered when the council started clearing the property for redevelopment and could have been lying there undiscovered for over two years.*

Officers investigating the case now say they believe the body is that of homeless man Steven Hetherington, who disappeared from his hometown in Warwickshire over four years ago. A family friend is quoted as saying the man suffered from mental health problems and left his home following a row with his father.

"It's very sad. It was his choice to cut himself off from his family. We have no idea how he ended up in Tewkesbury."

A private funeral will take place following the inquest.'

About the Author

Originally from Northumberland but now based in Northampton, Kris was a Civil servant for 20 years before retraining in the charity sector. She has worked for some wonderful charities, starting with the Motor Neurone Disease Association, and is currently working for a homeless charity in Northampton as well as volunteering at Northampton Hospital.

Kris is married with 3 lovely step daughters and 6 step-grandchildren. When not writing she likes to travel; particularly to see family in Sardinia and Belgium.

While writing Kris likes to listen to Scala radio and Classic FM.

Lightning Source UK Ltd.
Milton Keynes UK
UKHW010932170522
403116UK00002B/389